This Place Has
No Atmosphere

Also by Paula Danziger:

The Cat Ate My Gymsuit
The Pistachio Prescription
Can You Sue Your Parents for Malpractice?
There's a Bat in Bunk Five
The Divorce Express
It's an Aardvark-Eat-Turtle World

This Place Has No Atmosphere

Paula Danziger

91 - 221

Delacorte Press

Published by
Delacorte Press
Bantam Doubleday Dell Publishing Group, Inc.
666 Fifth Avenue
New York, N.Y. 10103

Library of Congress Cataloging in Publication Data
Danziger, Paula. [date of birth]
  This place has no atmosphere.

  Summary: Aurora loves her life on Earth in the
twenty-first century, until she learns that her
family is moving to the colony on the moon.
  [1. Moon—Fiction. 2. Moving, Household—
Fiction. 3. Science fiction]   I. Title.
PZ7.D2394Ti   1986   [Fic]
ISBN 0-385-29489-1
Library of Congress Catalog Card Number: 85–46070

Manufactured in the United States of America
October 1986
10   9   8   7   6   5   4
BVG

To Don and Ann Farber
Whose place does have atmosphere
And whom I love very much

Acknowledgments

Harris and Marijo Mallon-Breiman; Annie, Chris, and Rosie Flanders; June Foley; Pat Giff; Susie Haven; Nancy Kafka; Holly Morris; Elyse Myller; Lois Myller; Nicky Nicholson; Francine Pascal; Buzzy Tischler; Jane Traum

1 _____

"I think he likes you," Juna whispers, as Matthew sits down at the other end of the table and smiles at me.

"Shh." I look down at the school lunch of mystery meat and lumpy mashed potatoes. "Not so loud. If he hears you, I'll just die. . . . Anyway, he smiles at everyone. He's running for ninth-grade president."

As the rest of the group sits down at the table, the robot lunch monitor goes past our table, checking for litterers. It blinks its lights at Juna, who is blowing a straw wrapper at me from across the table.

"DETENTION." It makes a clicking sound at her. "This is the third time this week that you have been guilty of an infraction. Student 11481844, Juna Jamison, you will have to stay after school for three days."

Juna stares at the robot. "I guess that was the last straw for you."

The gang laughs.

The robot doesn't.

It hasn't been programmed to have a sense of humor.

The blinking lights change from red to black and

then back again. "RUDENESS. Now you have four days' detention."

Juna smiles at the robot. "Thank you. Want to flip a coin and make it double or nothing?"

"GAMBLING IS NOT PERMITTED ON SCHOOL PREMISES." The robot beeps and leaves as it spots a table of boys who are trying to make a pyramid out of Jell-O.

I look at Juna. "What did you do that for?"

She grins. "Randy Brock got a month's detention for using his telekinetic powers to put the vice-principal on the flagpole. I've been wanting to spend some time with him for a long while. Maybe now that we'll be in detention together, he'll notice me, even though he's a senior and I'm only a freshman."

"Couldn't you have just smiled at him in the hall or something?" Cosmosa Lloyd asks, as she takes the cellophane off a dish of peaches drowned in juice.

"I tried that already. Now it's time for more drastic measures." She touches her hair. "I heard that his favorite singer is Rita Retrograde."

That explains why Juna looks the way she does.

Rita Retrograde has straight one-inch long hair on the right side of her head and shoulder-length curly hair on the other side. It is dyed purple on the right side and pink on the left. It is tipped with liquid silver and is braided throughout with tiny light bulbs.

So is Juna's.

Her parents had a fit.

I bet Rita Retrograde's parents weren't ecstatic either.

I know that my parents would have a cosmic cow if

I did that to myself. Maybe I should do it just to drive them nuts. But actually I liked Juna's hair better the old way too.

"You should have seen my mother's face when I walked in the door. Maybe she'll be so angry that I won't have to be in the Macy's Thanksgiving Day parade." The light bulbs in Juna's hair flash on and off as she talks.

Juna's a celebrity because she was the first child conceived in space. Her parents were honeymooning astronauts on a space shuttle expedition. When they came back to earth, Mrs. Jamison was pregnant. Ever since then, Juna's had lots of publicity. But lately she's become kind of embarrassed that the whole world knew what her parents were doing when the cameras were off. Now there are lots of kids not only started in space but born there. But Juna was the first, so she's in the news, kind of like back in the old days when the first test tube baby was born.

"Couldn't you just have told your parents that you didn't want to ride on the float this year?" I look at her, even though the blinking lights are beginning to drive me nuts.

"They never listen." She sighs. "My mother's really getting to me. What does she know about being a teenager? She hasn't been one for years. It's 2057 . . . and she was born decades ago."

Juna rants about her parents for a few more minutes, and then the rest of the gang starts complaining about their parents.

While they do, I think about how I feel about mine. Even though they're always telling me how much they love me, I really doubt it. They talk about it, but don't really show me that they mean what they say. Even when I try to please them, it never seems like I can. I hate to think about it because I get so upset.

Instead, I look around at the group that I'm part of, the Turnips.

The Turnips. We're one of the big groups at school. One of the kid's parents gave us the nickname and it stuck. That's because we always "turn up" at places, like to make appearances, hang out. I once heard someone say that we turn up like bad pennies and that we turn up our noses at kids who aren't cool enough.

The kid who made that comment was someone who tried to get into the group and didn't make it.

It's a weird thing, groups. At our school, if you're not in one, you're a nobody. It's kind of gross, actually. Sometimes I think that the only reasons I got into the Turnips are that my house is in the right neighborhood, a lot of kids think I'm kind of cute, and I'm in a lot of school plays. Secretly, though, I'm not always so sure I fit in. It's a good thing that I can act, so that no one notices.

Most of the people in our neighborhood have lots of money; not my family, though. My parents work for the government—in the Medical Department. They've made lots of important discoveries, so the government has rewarded them with use of the house we live in. It's a very big-deal bonus. So there we are, and I am part of the group.

"Look at the ugly tunic Miranda Cummings is wearing," Cosmosa says. "I wouldn't be caught dead in that outfit. It should be used to wipe up birdcage droppings."

I look.

Miranda's at the other side of the cafeteria, talking to some kids.

Her outfit is not so bad.

I think Cosmosa just doesn't like her because Miranda got on the yeardisk staff and Cosmosa didn't.

It reminds me of the time, years ago, that I wanted to be friends with Tandy Connors and Cosmosa told me I shouldn't be seen hanging out with creeps or people would think I was one, too.

Cosmosa can be really mean when she wants to be, and a lot of the kids follow her lead, so I stopped seeing Tandy, even though I hated myself for it.

Sometimes I wonder what would happen if I wasn't part of the group, but mostly I've learned to just fit in, and I'm happy—I guess. Juna really is a terrific best friend, and a lot of the kids are really nice, when you talk to them one to one.

Thinking of really nice kids, I sneak a look at Matthew.

He's definitely grown up a lot over the summer.

We'd look good as a couple.

He's about six inches taller than my 5'6", with brown curly hair, gray eyes, and long eyelashes.

I've got blond straight hair, greenish eyes, and short eyelashes, which would be much longer if my parents would let me have a lash transplant.

I asked them for one but they said that my friends and I are too concerned with appearances instead of important things. They said that if I devoted as much

time to my schoolwork as I do to my looks I would be
a straight-A student, instead of a B one. I asked them
if I got straight A's, would they let me have the lash
transplant. Their answer was NO, so Matthew has
longer lashes than I do and I still have a B average.

Juna blows a straw wrapper at me to get my attention.

She gets three more days of detention.

I look at her.

"It's time to get ready for class," she reminds me.

We empty our garbage into the disposal hole in the
center of the table.

I watch as it disappears through a tube that leads to
the basement, where the automatic trash compactor
mushes it into tiny blocks, which are later trans-
formed into a power source.

This process is a fairly new development. Everyone seems to be amazed that garbage is being used to
run the school, but I don't see what's so unusual
about that. The same can be said about Mr. Finsterwald, the principal.

Putting the dirty dishes and the tray on the con-
veyer belt, I rush to my favorite class, Drama of the
Twenty-first Century.

Juna's taking Building Your Own Synthesizer.

I've even found out what Matthew's schedule is.
He's got BESP—Beginning Extrasensory Perception.
If he's doing well in it, he should know how much I
want to go out with him.

I rush into class and sit down in my seat, careful to
put my thumbprint on the attendance-taking square
on the desk so that I'm not marked late or absent.

I think about Matthew and how my life would be complete if he asked me out and fell in love with me.

There's about as much chance of that happening, though, as there is of my living on the moon.

2

"You'd think that by the twenty-first century some-one would have invented a zit zapper." Juna stares in the store window and frowns at a pimple-squeeze mark on her chin. "Gross. I'm so gross."

"No, you're not." I look at her. "Just stop touching it."

"How's Randy ever going to fall in love with some-one who looks like a tube of leaking mayonnaise?" Juna wails.

"That's so disgusting," I tell her. "Look, Juna, it's one pimple. You're not a living pus bomb."

"You're just saying that because you're my best friend." She puts her hand across the lower part of her face.

"Let's go to Vid-Sound," I suggest, to get her mind on something else. "They have Rita Retrograde's new holograph, 'Robot Love.'"

We step onto a moving sidewalk.

As it moves toward the store, I look around.

The Monolith Mall is so wonderful.

We're on the fifteenth floor, the one where most of the junior and senior high kids hang out.

There are one hundred and forty-four floors at the Monolith.

The top twenty are for recreation and are taken care of by the government. They are there to make up for the loss of public land that was sold to private industries by politicians years ago. The space is really great. There are swimming pools, roller- and ice-skating rinks, hiking trails, a zoo, a bird sanctuary. My parents say it used to be better when the wilderness was outside the malls, but how should I know?

Forty floors are filled with stores.

Condominiums and cooperative apartments are on the rest.

There are all these stories about people who spend their whole adult lives in malls . . . living . . . working . . . playing. They never leave. "Mole Minds" is what my parents call them.

I really wouldn't mind living in the mall, but my parents go nuts whenever I mention it. We live in a real house now, but soon single houses may have to come down to make room for environmental hives. My parents have been very active in a group that's collected petitions and stuff, but it doesn't seem to be working. There are just so many people.

Getting off the moving stairs, Juna and I go into Vid-Sound. We're given a token, which allows us to spend ten minutes listening in a special preview booth. Entering the booth, we put the token in and slip the disk into the machine and watch as Rita holographically appears in the booth with us as the music plays around us. A robot image appears also, doing the latest dance, the vertebration-automation. It's the ultimate.

After the time's up, Juna and I look around the store for a while.

"I'm getting these." Juna picks out four viddisks.

She's so lucky. Her family is rolling in megabucks. After her parents left the space program, they invested in taxicopters and made a mint. Juna's allowance is about five times what mine is. Even though she's always complaining, they give her just about everything she wants.

There are two viddisks that I really crave. "The Quarks in Concert at the Astrodome" is one. It's this group of really cute guys who play a combination of synthesizers and petri dishes. The other is by the Jackson 127, descendents of a group once called the Jackson Five.

"I'll lend you the money," Juna says. "Don't worry about when you can pay it back."

"But I already owe you for the T-shirt that I bought last week." I remember that T-shirt and think about how I don't even like it anymore.

"Don't worry so much." Juna smiles. "You're my best friend. What are best friends for?"

I look at the disks and think about the fight my mother and I had this morning. She said that I couldn't have a bigger allowance until my attitude showed some improvement and that I had to have a curfew on school nights. When I tried to explain that "everyone else is allowed to stay out late," she said, "You're not everyone else."

It makes me so angry that I can't even deal with it.

I decide to buy the disks to make myself happy.

Borrowing the money from Juna, I say, "Don't worry. I'll pay you back soon. My grandmother will give it to me."

I'm almost sure that's positively true, but even if she doesn't give me the money, I'll be really nice to my parents and they'll give me an advance. Sneaky, but it usually works.

We leave the store and get back on the moving sidewalk. Juna says, "Let's look at that store window," and we step off again.

The live models in the window are wearing new "mood clothes," made up of fabrics that change color according to how the wearer feels and what the wearer is doing.

Some other kids from school are also looking in the window.

One is Brandonetta Simmons, who is wearing Walkperson earrings, tuned to a frequency that only she can hear. I don't think there's been more than a year of her life when she wasn't wired for music. It's very hard to hold a conversation with her, since she sings her replies.

"Look there," Juna whispers and points. "Ralph Norton. Yecch."

Juna and Ralph have not done well together since seventh grade, when our science teacher mentioned the big bang theory and Ralph made a comment about Juna's parents.

He spots us and comes over.

"Hi, Aurora."

I nod and look at the mood clothes.

"Hello, Space Cadet." He looks at Juna. "I'm surprised that someone doesn't put you on a space ship until your hair gets back to normal. Isn't there a law against eye pollution?"

Juna glares at him. "Why don't you go away before I throw up on your slimy body?"

Ralph turns to me and says, "She really loves me. You know that, don't you? Throwing up is not what she really wants to use my body for."

As he walks away, I look at Juna.

She's blushing, really blushing. Actually, the pink of her skin goes well with the colors of her hair.

I start to giggle.

"It's not funny." She pretends to stick her finger down her throat. "He's so awful."

I nod.

"Look, I'm going to go hang out at the soda kiosk. I've made a list of all of Randy's hangouts and that's one of them. Want to come with me?"

I shake my head. "No, thanks. I'll stay here and watch the clothes change color for a while, unless you think you'll need protection from Norton."

"No. I'll be okay. He's a creepster, but harmless." She grins. "I can take care of myself."

After she leaves, I look at the dancing models.

Their mood clothes are like rainbows, except for one gray tunic that never changes. The model is obviously not having a great day.

I feel someone's hand on my shoulder and turn around.

It's Matthew. "Hi, Aurora. Want to go for an ice cream or something?"

I nod.

I'm glad that I'm not wearing mood clothes right now.

I'm not sure what color "nervous" would be.

3

The counterman wipes his hands on a towel. "What flavor do you kids want?"

"It's hard to decide." I look at the huge list of flavors and toppings. "I guess I'll have a scoop of vanilla with sprinkles."

"Boring," Matthew says.

I pretend to pull a knife out of my heart. "Boring? Well, excuse me."

Matthew gives his order: banana, rocky road, cherry cheesecake, and praline ice cream—mixed with M&M's and Oreos with nuts on top.

The counterman punches the choices into the computer in front of him, and the combination comes out of the machine and into a cup.

We pay and walk over to a table.

On the way, I see our reflections in a mirror.

I do like the way we look together.

Sitting down, he takes a spoonful of ice cream.

It's hard to feel shy when the person you're nervous around has accidentally put a smudge of Oreo on his nose.

I reach over and remove the gunk from his face with my napkin.

He smiles. "Thanks. When I was a little kid, I always had a milk mustache on my face."

I nod. "Me too. My mother used to say I looked good in the food I wore—especially linguini with red clam sauce."

We eat our ice cream silently for a few minutes, then I start to giggle.

Matthew looks at me questioningly.

I giggle more. Once I get started, it's hard to stop, but I try to, since I don't want him to think I'm laughing at him. "With all the flavors at this place, I started to think about what would happen if they ran out of names. Then I thought of lizard lemon and fingernail fudge."

"Yecch." Matthew laughs. "How about toejam tofu."

"Nicotine nectarine."

By the time we quit, we've added owl pellet peach, mucous mocha, snot sundae, phlegm frappe, and cow-chip chip to the list.

It's so disgusting that I can't finish my vanilla with sprinkles.

Matthew finishes mine and then says, "Aurora, I want to know two things. First of all, you don't go out with Joandrew anymore, do you?"

I shake my head. Joandrew and I broke up over the summer when he started hanging out with a group of dopers. They were really pond scum. He changed so much. I tried to help him see how awful that drug scene was, how he was frizzling his brains, but he wouldn't listen. After staying up every night crying and worrying, I finally told him that he had to make a choice—me or drugs. He made the choice. I've heard that he's had to go into a drug rehab program. I'm sorry, but I really don't want to have anything to do with him anymore.

"No, I don't," I say to Matthew.

"Good." He smiles at me. "My second question, then, is, Want to go to the homecoming dance with me?"

The homecoming dance, "Evening on Jupiter." All the announcements say it will be "absolutely out of this world." I've been hoping that Matthew would ask me to it. He really is the nicest boy I know.

"Yes. I would love to go with you." I'm so happy.

"They'll have announced the election results that afternoon. I'll know if I've won or lost."

"Either way"—I touch his hand—"I'll be very happy to be with you."

He reaches over and holds my hand. "I'm glad. I've liked you since second grade, when you refused to use a coloring book and drew all over the walls."

"Mr. Talbot certainly didn't like me after that." I smile, remembering how I had to stay after to clean it up. I was so angry. "But Matthew, why didn't you ever let me know that you liked me?"

He shrugs. "You've always had so many boyfriends. I guess that it's just taken a while to get up my nerve."

"Seven years, though."

"I had to get taller." He grins. "And anyway, now

that I'm taking BESP, I kind of figured out that maybe you like me." He looks proud of himself.

"I'll tell your teacher to give you an A." I smile at him. "You're right."

A girl comes up to the table, someone from school whom I've seen around but don't know.

She nods at me, then turns to Matthew. "You've got my vote. I like your stand on using fewer computers and more people in the Guidance Department."

Matthew smiles and says, "Thanks. I appreciate your vote and will do my best."

I feel invisible for a minute. I wonder if the President's husband felt this way during the last government election.

Finally she leaves.

I debate batting my eyelashes at Matthew to look cute and sexy but decide against it. First of all, they're too short. Second of all, I think Matthew knows that I'm here.

We walk back to the store window so that I can find Juna.

She's watching the models.

As Matthew and I hold hands, we smile at each other.

If I had mood clothes on right now, they would be every shimmery color of the spectrum.

4 _____

"So you really like this new boyfriend of yours?"
Grandma Jennifer takes a pan of brownies out of the
oven. "His name is Matthew, right?"

I nod. "Oh, Grandma, I really do. He's so nice . . .
and cute . . . and fun."

She smiles. "I remember when I was your age, I
used to love falling in love. You and I are a lot alike."

I stick my fingers into the pan. "Ow, that's hot. I
burned myself."

Grandma Jennifer breaks off a leaf from the aloe
plant and puts the sap on my burned fingers. "Be
careful. You always want things immediately. Try to
wait. The brownies won't run away."

I blow on my fingers. "But I love them when
they're hot and gushy . . . when you can sort of roll
them warm into balls.

"Me too." She kisses my forehead. "When your
mother was a little girl, she liked them cooled off and
refrigerated.

"Mom and I are so different." I sigh. "You and I are
more alike."

Grandma Jennifer nods. "It's true. But Aurora, remember that your mother loves you."

"She's got a funny way of showing it." I pick the brownie up with a spoon and blow on it. "Both of my parents have a funny way of showing it."

She says, "They do care. Sometimes I think they are so involved with work that they forget to let you know how much they care. But I know they do. And Aurora, try to understand them. They have done such important things in medicine, saved so many lives, won so many awards. Other doctors and dentists, from all over the world, come here to observe them at work. I'm so proud. You should be too. I know that you and Starr are very important parts of their lives."

"But they are just so busy that sometimes it seems like they only notice me when there's a problem." I shake my head. "Just living with them is a problem for me. And they like Starr much better than they like me."

My grandmother smiles. "They understand her interests better, but they do love you too."

I love my grandmother and usually agree with her, but this time I think she's just being loyal to her daughter and doesn't realize how much I hurt.

Grandma Jennifer and I take another spoonful of warm brownie.

Our mouths are soon full.

I feel so comfortable being with her.

"You know what I like even better than brownies like this?" she asks. "I like the brownie mix before it's baked."

"Me too."

"Aurora, when you called, you said you wanted to come over and ask me something. What is it?"

I look down at the floor. "I hate to ask."

She takes my hand. "Are you in trouble?"

I shake my head. "Not *big* trouble . . . just money again. I owe some to Juna and I've overspent my allowance."

"Again." She says softly.

I nod, feeling embarrassed.

She sits quietly for a few minutes and then says, "I thought this is what it was all about. Every month, you've asked for money and I've given it to you. It worries me that this keeps happening."

"I'm sorry."

"Don't be sorry," she says. "Just realize what you're doing. When you're unhappy, you buy yourself something. Then you're unhappy because you owe money."

"But then I'm happy when you help me out."

"I know." She sighs. "But then it starts all over again. I want to help, but I'm not sure that what I've been doing is helping."

Panic. What am I going to do if Grandma Jennifer doesn't come through? I'll have to ask my parents, and that'll be a rough scene.

"Grandma," I plead. "Please. I'll be good. I promise."

She kisses me on the forehead. "You are good. You're just having a problem, and I want to help in the best way possible. Let me figure out what I should do."

She thinks.

I sit there and wait.

Finally she says, "I'll give you the money this time, and then you'll do something for me to pay off the debt."

I jump up and hug her. "Thank you. Thank you."

"This is the last time," she warns.

I nod. "It'll never happen again."

She hugs me. "I want you to try to work out your problems."

"I hate to think about them."

"That's one of the problems that you'll have to work out."

I take a spoonful of brownie and put it in her mouth.

She smiles at me with brownie all over her lips. "Don't try to change the subject."

I grin at her.

She says, "About the job . . ."

"Yes?"

She looks at me. "Your job will be to spend an entire day with your mother trying to get along with her."

"Grandma!"

"Don't Grandma me. I want you to try."

"Oh, okay." It's my turn to sigh. "She's been offering to spend a Saturday with me for a while. I always make excuses, but I guess I could give up going to the mall this week and do it."

Oh, yuck.

"I'm so glad," Grandma says. "I just want you to try. I won't expect miracles. Trust me. I know that relations between mothers and daughters are not always easy."

Neither of us speaks for a few minutes. Then she says, "Tell me about the Turnips. What's new?"

It's so much fun to tell her about the stuff that happens at school. I don't tell her everything, but I do tell her a lot. "The group's new motto is, The Turnips can't be beet!"

"So what's the latest?" Grandma really loves the news.

I tell her about the P.T. Meechies. Over a week and a half ago signs began to appear on display monitors, in the halls, and even on a dittoed test paper. The signs said things like "The P.T. Meechies are coming," "The P.T. Meechies are arriving," and "Get ready for the P.T. Meechies." No one knew what was happening, and then one day the boys in the Turnips showed up at school wearing very ugly ties that they bought at a mall sale. They talked about what mooches they are, how they always come over to people's houses and eat everything in sight. The P.T. Meechies have arrived.

Grandma Jennifer laughs.

So do I.

She's so terrific.

So's Grandpa Josh.

I only wish that I felt this good at home.

5 _____

Sometimes I think that there was a mistake in the birthing room and that Mom and Dad brought home the wrong baby.

My parents say that's impossible since they were both present at my birth and watched as the identidisk was implanted on my shoulder blade.

They do agree that otherwise they'd also wonder if there'd been a switch.

We're all so different.

My parents don't care about fashion, saying that their old-fashioned mylar jumpsuits are good enough. It's so embarrassing to be seen with them. Half the time they just wear their doctor and dentist uniforms.

They'd like it if I'd be more academic and less social. I have tried to please them. When they wanted me to take computer lessons, I did. After I learned, I used my new skills to break into fifteen bulletin boards to leave the message "Aurora loves Albie." I thought that would impress Albie. He said it made him want to puke. I guess girls are more mature than boys are in the third grade. Somehow I don't think my parents were overwhelmed about my chances for a career in computeronics.

The only thing my whole family agrees on is exercise.

Today's the day I'm spending with my mother to pay back Grandma Jennifer. But my mother has no idea that's why I'm doing it.

We're on our exercycles in our fitness room.

I'm really going to try to make this day a good one.

"Mom, how old were you when you knew you were in love with Dad?" I pedal quickly.

She stops looking at the video projection wall, at the ongoing scene of an old-fashioned mountain road, and stares at me. "I had a crush on him when I was thirteen years old."

"My age."

"But we didn't even date until your dad became the dentist at the holistic wellness center where I was interning. That was after we had both devoted time to our studies and were fully developed individuals."

"How could you be fully developed individuals if you didn't let yourself fall in love?"

She shakes her head. "Aurora, you just don't take things seriously enough—not the important things. Anyway, your father and I met again and we fell in love. Why are you asking? You know all this already."

"I love stories about love." I sigh.

My mother smiles. "You're going to tell me that Matthew's your true love, right? Honey, you said that about Joandrew and Michael and Doug and Phil and Albie and Cliff and Julio."

"Mom, Julio was in preschool," I remind her.

"You sent out wedding invitations as soon as you learned to print," she reminds me.

We laugh.

"Let's change the biking scenery," my mother suggests.

"Okay. Let's push the shore button."

She does, and all of a sudden it's like we're riding on a sandy beach, with rolling waves and the sound of birds overhead.

We ride for a while.

It's so nice and peaceful.

I say, "Next week is cheerleading tryouts. I know that you think it's silly of me to want to be a cheerleader, but everyone says I have a really good chance to be on the squad, and I'm excited."

My mother says nothing for a few minutes. Then she stops her exercycle.

"Aurora, I have something to tell you." She doesn't look happy. "Your dad and I were going to wait to tell you and Starr when we were positive, but since it's probably going to happen, I think it's only fair to prepare you now."

I stop my bike. "What is it? What are you talking about?"

"Honey"—she gets off her exercycle and comes over to mine—"your father and I have the opportunity to use our skills in a very special, very wonderful way. We've been offered new positions and will probably take them."

"What does that mean?"

She hesitates. "It means . . . that the family is going to have to move. But it's going to be a wonderful opportunity for all of us."

"Move?" I whisper.

She reaches over and touches my hair. "It's far."

"How far?" My stomach begins to hurt.

She doesn't say anything for a minute.

I start to have terrible thoughts. What if we have to move far away . . . out of the state or even out of the country. . . . I know that my parents are always getting job offers from all over.

"How far?" I repeat.

"Honey"—she reaches over and touches my hair—"it's far. We're going to be pioneers. We're going to move to the colony on the moon."

The moon.

"Do Grandma Jennifer and Grandpa Josh know about this?" I ask.

"No. We didn't want them to try to talk us out of it."

The moon.

I don't believe it.

I'll just refuse to go.

I don't believe it.

I wish that the shore video and the bike were real. If they were, I'd drive right into the ocean.

6 _____

School is going on as if the world as I know it has not ended.

The Turnips are sad, but they haven't stopped breathing from the shock.

I was kind of hoping that they would storm my house and hold a sit-in and refuse to leave until my parents changed their minds. They didn't. Juna and Matthew care the most—the rest seem most interested in turning up for my going-away party.

It makes me feel a little sad that they don't care more.

The school intercom clicks on and Mr. Finsterwald begins the announcements.

1. "EVERYONE MUST HAVE MORE SCHOOL SPIRIT."

Juna slumps down in her desk, pretending to snore.

2. "ALL SENIORS ARE TO MAKE AND KEEP APPOINTMENTS TO BE VIDEOTAPED FOR YEARDISK PICTURES."

Finsterwald reminds us that it's an innovation and

a privilege to have permanent videos of school life to look at forever. He stresses that suitable attire is necessary and *no* attire will mean suspension from school.

Juna giggles. "I kind of liked last year's pictures of Terrence Bradman and Larry Ardville."

Terry followed Finsterwald's order that all senior boys wear ties. Of course, that's all he wore—a fluorescent tie.

Larry, on the other hand, was totally dressed. The only problem was that the clothes he wore were made out of clear plastic wrap.

Last year's senior class is a legend in the history of Alan Shepard High School.

It makes me laugh to think about them until I realize that my parents have pledged five years of time on the moon. I won't be back in time to graduate with my class or to be in the yeardisk. They won't even let me stay with my grandparents or with Juna's family.

3. "THERE WILL BE AN AFTER-SCHOOL MEMORIAL SERVICE FOR MR. ED, THE BIOTECH CLASS GERBIL, WHO DIED FROM CONCUSSION COMPLICATIONS SUFFERED WHEN HE TOOK A WRONG TURN IN THE MAZE."

"He was cute," Juna says. "We should go."

I remind her that she still has detention.

4. "THE PERSON OR PERSONS WHO BROKE INTO THE SCHOOL COMPUTER SYSTEM AND CHANGED ALL OF THE SENIORS' GRADES TO A'S WILL BE PROSECUTED AS

SOON AS CAUGHT. THE SYSTEM IS NOW
BACK IN WORKING ORDER."

Darn it. Everyone was looking forward to a gradu-
ation with three hundred and forty-two valedicto-
rian speeches.

5. "TRYOUTS FOR THE SCHOOL PLAY, CATS,
BATS, RATS, AND GNATS, WILL BE HELD NEXT
WEEK."

Oh, no. That's what I really wanted more than
anything else—to be in the high school play. When I
first got to Shepard, the drama coach came up and
said that she'd seen me in the junior high play and
that she was looking forward to working with me.
Now we never will, because I have to go to the moon.
I don't know what I want to do more: die or kill my
parents. Either way, though, I still couldn't be in the
play. It's so not fair. Being in a play is something that
I'm good at and really care about doing.

Mr. Finsterwald is droning on over the loudspeaker about the need for more discipline.

Someone throws a paper airplane.

Juna.

Someone hits the intercom speaker with a paper
space shuttle.

The homeroom teacher.

"AND NOW FOR A SPECIAL PRINCIPAL ANNOUNCE-
MENT."

Mr. Finsterwald reminds us how lucky we all are
that the administration allows students to have
homecoming week with such events as Jet Set Tennis
Day, Come As a Martian Day, and Walk Backwards
Afternoon. He is very angry about Come As You

Were Day—yesterday—when students dressed as past reincarnations or as they were when they were little. It seems that someone stole the Student Council president's Cabbage Patch robot.

It must be returned by the end of the day . . . or else.

Mr. Finsterwald isn't quite clear on what "or else" means in this case, but then he never is.

The bell rings, signaling the end of homeroom—not a moment too soon.

I rush out of homeroom.

Matthew's waiting for me.

As we walk down the hall, he has his arm around my shoulder.

Juna is at her locker, trying to find her elementary geoalgebra homework.

Kids say hello to me.

It's going to be very hard to leave.

7

Ways to Keep From Going to the Moon

1. Get married.
2. Get pregnant.
3. Pretend that I have amnesia and don't recognize my parents anymore.
4. Hide out at the Monolith Mall until I'm of age.
5. Fall to the ground, grab my parents' legs, and plead with them to change their minds.
6. Promise to be nice to Starr for forty-three years.
7. Discuss in a logical grown-up way how I will hold my breath until my parents give in.
8. Promise not to ask for clothes for at least two years. (I better be more realistic and make it three months—or maybe one.)
9. Promise to take all of my veggie-vitamins.
10. Pretend to sleepwalk so that they'll be afraid to trust me on the space ship.
11. Make believe I have shuttlephobia and will have a major freakout once the doors close.
12. Promise not to watch my television wristwatch until my homework is finished.

13. Get my grandparents to convince their children not to leave. (After all, if I have to listen to my parents, they should have to listen to theirs.)
14. Remind the parents that they aren't the only ones involved in the move—that even though Starr, the creepling traitor, says that she likes the idea, she's not the only kid in the family.
15. Beg.
16. Cry.
17. Scream.
18. Faint.
19. Refuse to go.

It's no use. Kids have no say. Tomorrow night's our going-away party.

Some party.

8 _____

They'll be sorry someday.

I'll become a universe-famous actress, win an Oscar, and tell the world that my parents deserve absolutely, positively no thanks at all.

Then when I have kids, I'll tell the children that their grandparents were eaten by aliens, even if my parents are still alive.

I'll pretend that I'm a full-term test tube baby who never knew who her parents were.

I'll fall into a moon crater and suffocate on lunar dust, and everyone will blame my parents.

It's no use.

It's just no use.

Sitting on my bed, I look around my room. All the posters are off the wall, to be stored for the five years that we are supposed to be gone. By the time we return, most of the groups won't even be popular anymore.

I can't even take my collection of plays with me. They're antiques, real books, given to me at Christmas by my grandparents. "Too heavy. Store it," my father told me. "You can look up anything you'll need on the computer and get a printout if you want." He just doesn't understand anything that's not scientific. It's not the same to have a printout as the real book.

I also can't take all my clothes with me. Two suitcases each—that's all we can take to the moon. New moon clothes will be "issued" to us when we get there. I've lent most of my stuff to Juna, who has promised to wear some of my clothes each day, so that part of me is at Alan Shepard High as long as my class is there.

I've cried so much in the past few days.

The tears start again.

There's a knock at the door.

"Aurora, the company's arriving. I want you to come downstairs." It's my father.

"Go away," I yell. "I'm not going to a party to celebrate my having to go away from a place that I don't want to leave."

He opens the door and comes in.

I pretend that he's not there.

He steps over the boxes filled with all my stuff that's to be put in storage and sits down on the chair next to my bed. He doesn't even move the stuffed animals that I'm putting into storage. It's a shame that they don't bite.

"Aurora." He leans over and moves my hair from in front of my eyes. "Honey, believe us. We don't want you to be so unhappy."

"If you didn't want me to be so unhappy, you wouldn't move just when I've started high school and love it," I cry.

He sighs. "We've been through this already, so many times. Mom and I can make a real contribution on the moon. It's such an honor to be chosen, and our research will open new frontiers in medicine. We'll be able to try out new techniques and experiment with the manufacture of new medicines while in orbit and while on the moon."

I feel like my heart is going to break. Maybe my mother should do a transplant on me and put in an artificial heart or at least one that isn't in so much pain.

He continues. "We also want to get you kids away from pollution, overcrowding, and values that we don't like. We only want what's best for all of us. Surely you understand that."

"Not best for all of us—*you!*" I pull at a thread on the bedspread. "Daddy, please let me stay here."

"No." He frowns. "Remember the first time you stayed overnight at Juna's. You were so homesick that we had to pick you up at three o'clock in the morning —you, your teddy bear, and your binkie."

"Daddy, I was six years old," I remind him. "I've stayed over at Juna's house a zillion times since then. I don't take my teddy bear with me any more, and my binkie got shredded in the wash years ago. And I promise you, I'm not going to call you to pick me up to take me to the moon."

He stands up. "We understand how hard this is for you. Don't think that we don't. However, all things considered, we are going to the moon as a family— because we *are* a family. Your mother and I have agreed that if it's absolutely unbearable for you after a year, then we'll reconsider. And maybe let you return and stay with Grandma and Grandpa, even though we hate the idea of breaking up the family."

Five years. Even a year seems like an eternity. And a year from my life is a higher percentage of time than a year out of my father's life. Even I can figure that out.

"Daddy, please."

He shakes his head sadly. "Honey, be reasonable. There's company downstairs. Take ten minutes to pull yourself together and join us."

After he leaves, I feel like throwing one of my squashed animals at the closed door, but decide not to take it out on them.

Instead I slam my hand into a pillow and for fifteen minutes think about possible disasters that could befall him that I couldn't be blamed for.

Even though no life as we know it has been discovered in outer space, I hope that there is such a thing as a giant lunar lizard. And I hope that it eats my father—slowly, chomping on him with sharpened steel fangs, oozing lizard glob all over his body, breathing terrible slimy lizard breath on him during his last horrible moments.

After the monster's done with my father, he can have my mother and sister for dessert.

There's a knock on my door.

This time it's my mother.

My parents like to alternate knocks on the door.

She comes in and stands there with her hands on her hips. "Everyone wants to see you. Come downstairs *right now* and act like a human being. You don't want to spend the entire evening in this room and miss saying good-bye to everyone. Just think of how unhappy you'll be if we leave for the training center and you haven't said good-bye. Juna and Matthew and the rest of your friends are downstairs already."

I stare at her.

She's trying to sound calm, but I can tell that she's not happy. "It's up to you. It's your choice. Come down now or stay up here."

What a choice, I think. Giving in to them and joining the party as if everything's okay or not having a chance to see my friends one last time.

I relent. "I'll go downstairs."

She smiles. "That's my girl. And remember, no long face. You don't want to turn this party into a disaster."

When we get downstairs, my mother puts her arm around my shoulder.

I stand stiffly.

What I really want to do is yell and scream, but I can't. Parents have a way of not letting you get away with stuff like that.

Since I want to be an actress someday, I'll just pretend that this is all a play.

1.

ACT I. SCENE THE PARTY.
The heroine enters.

9

CHARACTERS

Aurora, *the heroine and wronged party*
The parents, *the villians*
Starr, *the sister and villainette*
Juna, *the best friend*
Matthew, *the boyfriend*
Grandma Jennifer, *a good person*
Grandpa Josh, *another good person*
Assorted Turnips, relatives, and neighbors

The entire action takes place in the Williams's house.

JUNA *(clapping her hands)*. She's here.

MATTHEW. I was afraid you'd never leave your room.
(He puts his arm around Aurora, who puts her head on his shoulder.)

Olivia (who gives new meaning to the word heliumhead) heads toward the group. On the way over, she trips over Brandonetta Simmons, who is swaying to the beat of her own music.

OLIVIA. Aurora, I'm so sorry you're leaving.

AURORA. Me too.

OLIVIA. Before you go, do you think you could teach me to do a triple cartwheel, ending in a headstand?

AURORA. We're leaving tomorrow. I don't think I'll have a chance.

OLIVIA. I just know if I could do that I'd make the squad—now that you're not going to be competing. *(She rushes off to see Gary, whom she has a crush on. He rushes off to avoid her.)*

JUNA. Well, that was disgusting. I don't see how she could remind you that you won't be able to be on the squad. Anyway, she doesn't have a chance anyway.

AURORA. During junior high tryouts, she tripped on her shoelaces and her only split was the one on her lip from when she fell on her face.

A robot waiter stops in front of them, offering health food. Almost everyone waits for the robot who is carrying junk food.

The doorbell rings. Grandma Jennifer and Grandpa Josh arrive. They were born during the late 1980s and early '90s and often talk about "the good old days." They can even remember when computers couldn't talk and when smoking cigarettes was still legal.

GRANDMA *(comes over and pats Aurora on the head)*. Darling, it's like cutting out my heart to have my family leave for the moon.

AURORA. My heart feels cut too.

FATHER *(joining group)*. Jenny, don't talk like that. You can get on the list and take the shuttle for a visit when there's an opening.

GRANDMA. Don't make it sound like it's right in the

neighborhood. You don't just say "I think I'll drop in on the moon today."

FATHER *(putting his arm around her).* We'll be back in five years. It's not forever.

GRANDMA *(clutching her heart).* Only five years. . . . I could be dead by then.

AURORA. Grandma, don't say that.

GRANDPA. She's healthier than any of us. Don't worry, honey. With all of the medical discoveries, we can expect to have a good chance to live to be a hundred. Anyway, you know that you've inherited your flair for dramatics from her.

GRANDMA. They can find a cure for cancer but they can't find a way to keep your family from moving to the moon.

FATHER. Jenny.

GRANDMA. Don't Jenny me. By the time you return, Aurora will be practically out of her teens. I'll miss seeing her through some of the most important years of her life . . . and Starr too. I'll miss seeing her go out on her first date.

AURORA *(sarcastically).* With the way Starr's social life seems to be shaping up, she probably will never even have a date on the moon . . . so it won't matter.

STARR. Ma, Aurora's being mean to me again.

AURORA. Not mean . . . truthful. That'll teach you to say that going to the moon is a great idea.

MOTHER. Girls! I don't want to hear any fighting on our last night all together.

Ralph Norton approaches. Juna exits. He follows.

MATTHEW *(noticing that tears are forming in*

Aurora's eyes). Aurora, let's go someplace where
we can be alone together.

*Matthew and Aurora walk into the backyard. They
stand in the moonlight and kiss . . . and kiss . . .
and kiss. There are sounds of the party in the back-
ground: people talking and laughing, Grandma
Jenny crying, the robot waiters crashing into each
other.*

MATTHEW. I'm going to miss you a lot.

AURORA. I'll miss you too.

MATTHEW *(kissing her on the neck, knowing there
will be a hickey there tomorrow to remember him
by).* I wish you didn't have to go.

AURORA. I'll be back in five years. We could wait for
each other.

Damn, I think. This is not a play. This is real life.
He's not going to wait five years. He already
waited to get tall. He probably won't even write after
the first month or so.

It's impossible. Here we are standing in the moonlight. By this time next month I'll have moved to the
place that's shedding its moonlight on other couples
. . . probably on Matthew and his new girl friend,
whoever she'll be.

By this time tomorrow, my family and I will be at
the training camp . . . our house rented out . . .
no Matthew, no Juna, no Turnips, no Grandma
Jenny, no Grandpa Josh . . . none of the people and
things I've known all my life . . . except my parents
and sister—and we're definitely not on each others'
favorites list this week.

No wonder I want to be an actress. Being anyone else is better than being me now.

If this were really a play, I feel like this should be

THE END.

10

"Are we almost there yet?" Starr whines for the nine hundredth time.

"No, we're not." My mother turns around in the front seat of the car. "Look, can't the two of you find something to occupy yourselves?"

"I'm not bothering anyone," I remind her.

"Well, you're the oldest," my mother reminds me. "Keep your sister company. Do something with her."

"What should I do with her?" I put my sunglasses on. "Teach her to dance? Pickle her?"

"Don't be fresh to your mother," my father orders. "Girls, look around on this trip. It's going to be almost your last chance to see earth for the next five years. When we come back, everything will be different."

Starr uses her sweet-child voice—"Okay, Daddy" —and looks out the window. In about three minutes, though, she flicks on her TV watch and checks out a favorite soap, *As the Earth Spins.*

I pretend to be asleep, but do look out the window. When you're wearing sunglasses, it's hard for parents to tell what you're doing. No way will I let them think

I'll do any more than I have to do—not after what they've done to me.

The car passes lots of new construction. All over the country, single houses are being torn down and environmental hives are being built. That's because there are many more people because of the last baby boom, which my father calls a "baby blast." Anyway, there are so many blasters now, as a result of births, test tubes, and cloning, that there's not a lot of room to live. (My father says that all that cloning around isn't funny and he's so upset by the situation that he won't even let me play Rita Retrograde's song "Send in the Clones.")

One of the reasons my parents love the idea of going to the moon is that there's not this kind of overcrowding.

Personally, I think that's because not a lot of people want to live on the moon.

I'm sick of hearing how privileged we are to be chosen.

"Look!" My father points. "There's the farm museum that we visited last year."

"May we see it again?" Starr looks up from her wristwatch. "I'd love to."

"Not enough time—as much as I'd love to stop." My father shakes his head. "The first training-camp session takes place tonight. We have to be there."

"What a shame." Starr pretends to be soooo disappointed, but I notice that she goes right back to watching her soap opera.

What a fake she is! It's my theory that in every

family of two or more kids, there's always the Goody Two-shoes and there's always the bad one.

We have, I guess, decided which is which in the Williams household.

"Cows, horses, pigs," my father says. "I remember when I was a kid there were still a lot of farms."

"Ones that grew their own food," my mother sighs.

I bet she's remembering her own garden, which had to be given up when it became illegal to own more land than what your house stood on. Zero lot lines, it's called.

Now there's no need for old-time farms, either, because of the invention of Agri-Culture, by which food and animals are manufactured in artificial mediums.

My father pulls into a rest area. "Pit stop."

We all get out of the car.

My parents hold hands for a minute and smile at each other.

Then Starr, Mom, and I go into the restaurant while my father stays outside to put a gas pellet into the compartment and to use the CAR-scan card computer.

I hope he enjoys using the car now while he can. There are no privately owned cars on the moon.

Starr, Mom, and I sit down at the table and punch our orders into the combination jukebox–food server. In a few seconds the music starts and our food arrives.

Mom starts another one of her heart-to-heart talks. She's big on that . . . but not so big on heart-to-heart listening.

"I really want to thank you girls for cooperating and agreeing to come to the moon."

We weren't allowed the choice, I think.

She nods. "I know."

It's not great having a mother who is very talented in reading minds. All people take the courses that the parapsychologists have developed, but some are better than others. My mother is one of the best. In fact, she's so good that she has had to learn to tune out a lot or she says that her brain would never rest or be focused. Maybe that's why she's so strong about what she says. Anyway, she doesn't block out what I think. I've worked hard at trying to keep my thoughts from her, but it's hard. She says she'll never abuse her power and get too deeply into my thoughts, but sometimes I wonder.

It's weird having a mother who doesn't listen but can read your mind.

She takes my hand. "Aurora . . . trust me. We really do know what's best for you and are sure that someday you will thank us for this experience."

Someday, I think, and don't care if she's tuned in.

She takes Starr's hand, too, and says, "By becoming settlers we will help all of humankind—not just because of your dad's and my work but also because of both of you. We're so proud that you've both agreed to be interviewed and tested. Just think how your input will help when Mars is settled."

My input about going to the moon is making me very unsettled.

11_____

Mr. "Call Me Buzz" Schwartz greets the group. "Welcome to CAMP, the training place for Coordinating American Moon Pioneers."

Chumps Are Moon Pioneers would be more accurate, I think, sinking further into the chair and looking around.

There are about a hundred people in the room . . . and not one of them is a cute boy my age.

In fact, there's only one boy who seems to be about my age, and he is what the old gang would refer to as a barfburger.

"Call Me Buzz" is busy introducing himself. "Years ago, before space travel was common, I was called an astronaut, kind of like in the really old days when people who operated airplanes were called aviators and then when there was nothing special about plane travel, they were just pilot and crew. That's the way it is now. I was an astronaut and now I'm a trainer at CAMP."

I wonder whether he knows Juna's parents. She once said that there's an organization of astronauts who get together and talk about the old days when people used to get airsick and stuff like that.

This one girl is taking notes. I think she's Barfburger's sister. At least she looks like they're related.

"Break up into groups of twenty-five," Buzz tells us. "Then introduce yourselves to each other."

I don't move. It's so scary to go into new groups.

My mother comes over and pinches me on the arm.

I move.

My parents and Starr go into three different groups.

I go to the group which does not have a member of my family in attendance.

Introductions begin.

The Mendez family, Mr. and Mrs. and their four-year-old quadruplets—Henny, Penny, Lenny, and Kenny—are first.

Mrs. Mendez says, "Little did I know that fertility drugs would turn into 'fourtility.' "

"Some days it feels like futility," Mr. Mendez says, as the quads do somersaults in the middle of the circle.

If there are not enough Mendez kids to start a sports team, at least they can be a cheerleading squad.

I wonder if the school on the moon has cheerleaders, or even a drama club.

Barfburger's name is Vern Verne. It figures.

His sister is Julie Verne.

They both seem so yucky.

Vern has so many pimples that he could be a crater map of the moon. What makes it totally disgusting is that he's always picking at them.

If that weren't vomitous enough, Vern has this awful laugh that sounds like a seal after he's caught a fish and is applauding himself—sort of a very deep voiced "Are. Are. Are."

Julie looks like a nerf ball with mousy brown hair. Not only does her hair look like that but she's always chewing on the end of it.

I wonder whether she ever coughs up hair balls.

Their parents are Agri-Culturists. It's natural that the Verne kids are such plants.

Emily Doowinkle, in a mood-sequined mini, is a member of Writers in Residence and will be conducting poetry classes on the moon.

The person in the group who looks the most interesting to me introduces herself. "I'm April Brown, a junior at Antioch College. My work-study year will take place on the moon. I'm so pleased and excited to be chosen."

She is dressed in a long lavender dress, with charm necklaces draped all the way to her waist. It's impossible to tell what all the charms are, but somehow I know that each one was specially chosen and that there's a great story about each of them. She also has different-color gemstones going up her multipierced earlobes. *91-221*

She looks really terrific and different. It's great to see someone so original.

Buzz joins our group and tells us that April has won

a nationwide essay contest and is the only person who will be staying for just one year.

Maybe I'll be able to go back the same time that she does. Then the trip back won't be so all alone.

Salvador Arply speaks next. He's this really weird-looking guy who has braided eyebrows and will be creating moon sculptures on a grant from the Universe Endowment of the Arts. "During the first years, most of the people sent to the moon were scientists, construction workers, miners, and manufacturers. Next came the support people—the families, the teachers. Now it's time for the arts. So here I am—to create, to teach."

I wonder whether actors will be sent to the moon.

Next, Buzz looks in my direction.

I look around.

It's me.

I'm next.

People are looking at me. Unless I'm on stage, that makes me nervous.

"Aurora Williams. My father's a dentist. My mother's a doctor. I have a younger sister, Starr."

"But who are *you?* Surely you are more than just a part of your family." Buzz sounds like one of my old psychology teachers.

I look around at the group. How can I tell these strangers who I am when I don't really know that myself?

It's so hard.

Where are the Turnips when I need them?

I hope April doesn't think I'm a blobbrain or anything.

Buzz doesn't give up. "How do you feel about going to the moon?"

"My parents want to go," I say.

"And you?" He continues.

Why do some grown-ups think they have the right to make kids tell everything in front of everyone?

I'd really like to say something like "They're making me go," but then maybe CAMP would tell us that it has to be voluntary and that I have a bad attitude and the family can't go. I can't let that happen. Last night my parents and I talked again and I promised to really try for them. I have to stick to it. I'm almost fourteen years old and that's really too young to leave home. Even though I want to sometimes, the thought of that is kind of frightening.

Buzz insists. "And what about you?"

"I go too. We're a package deal." I smile at him.

He nods and turns to the next person.

As the rest of the group introduce themselves, I think about how scary it would really be to leave my parents and how scary it is to be leaving my friends and the life that I have always known.

Sitting in a group of over one hundred people, I suddenly feel very alone.

12 _____

C.A.M.P. TEST   100%

NAME— *Aurora Borealis Williams*

T **F** 1. The moon is made of green cheese.

T F 2. The moon is a satellite of the earth and makes a 27-day orbit around the earth.

T **F** 3. The cow jumped over the moon long before Neil Armstrong first set foot there on July 20, 1969.

T **F** 4. There are three McDonald's stands on the moon and over 21 million MacMoon burgers have been sold there.

T F 5. The moon is about ¼ the size of Earth and weighs 180 billion trillion pounds (1/80 the weight of Earth).

T F 6. Tiny craters in rock surfaces are referred to as "zap pits."

T F 7. The light on the moon comes from the sun.

T F 8. The moon does not contain water.

T F 9. The moon's surface reaches 250° F during the daytime and cools to a frigid -250° F at night, due to lack of atmosphere. However, the environmental shield built over the moon colony protects the inhabitants.

T **F** 10. A crazy species of bug, found only on the moon, is called a lunar tic.

GIVE TWO FACTS THAT YOU HAVE LEARNED ABOUT THE MOON (one past, one present).

1. (Present) Fluids in the exposed human body will boil on the moon. In order not to become a hot dog, it will be wise to wear a space suit while not under the environmental shield.

2. (Past) "Fly man to the moon in this decade," was said by John F. Kennedy in the last century. [Contrary to popular opinion, it was not said by Spider Man, who was Fly Man's brother........ ..... just kidding! A.B.W.]

VERY FUNNY.
B.S.

I look at the comment on my test paper, which Buzz has just returned.

If my last initial were S, I'm not sure I'd like to have a nickname that begins with B.

"Now we're going to show you some historical film footage, and then we'll be giving you a tour of the space shuttle simulator," Buzz informs us.

One of the construction workers raises his hand.

"How come we have to go through all this? Why
can't we just go up to the moon right away? We don't
need all this historical and scientific information to
live and work someplace. I spent thirty years in Al-
toona without knowing much about it."

Buzz says, "The time here is important. It's not as if
you're going to be moving to a familiar environment
on this planet. You'll have to get used to new conditions, be prepared to live under an environmental
shield and have the commitment to stay on the moon
for at least five years under conditions that you won't
be used to. CAMP is the chance to train for that life.
It's also the chance for you and for us to make the
final decision about whether moon life will be right
for you."

I look at my parents.

They look back.

I read my father's lips. "We're going!"

Buzz looks at the group. "It's only two weeks. By
then most of you will be ready to go. . . . Also, a
new team is in final stages of training at the Johnson
Space Center, and the crew will be ready to fly in two
weeks."

Emily Doowinkle waves her hand.

"We're going to have to go up with a new team?
That makes me so nervous, I could just scream."

Being writer in residence, Emily rhymes everything.

She's so weird.

Buzz shakes his head. "Don't worry. They'll be
assisting our regular crew. We need more trained

personnel, since the Space Travel Program is growing in leaps and bounds."

Emily shakes her head.

"I wish about the shuttle, you wouldn't say leaps and bounds.

Language like that and my heart just pounds."

Buzz reassures her. "Don't worry. Let's just see the film about the very first man on the moon." He pushes the button on the giant screen monitor so that we can watch the film.

Just as the movie starts, the computoprojector breaks down.

Waiting for someone to get the machine to work, I practice writing backwards, which was what I always did when the projector at school broke down.

I love Matthew.

I look over and notice that Vern Verne has a runny nose. At least he's not picking that.

I really miss Matthew.

The projector is fixed.

"That's one small step for man, one giant leap for mankind," Neil Armstrong is saying.

Buzz explains how the line was later changed to add the article *a*, to make it "One small step for a man."

I wonder what Matthew is doing right this very second. He's the only man whose small step I'm interested in right now.

I also wonder what color(s) Juna's hair is this week.

I continue to practice writing backwards. Starr kicks at my foot to remind me to pay attention.

I stick my tongue out at her, but I listen to Buzz, who is telling us how the astronauts left stuff on the moon—a U.S. flag, a laser reflector, a seismometer, and a sheet of aluminum foil.

Litterbugs, I think.

It's not enough that we mess up our own planet; we leave junk on the first place we land.

Buzz says, "Now it's time for another simulation exercise."

He reminds us of the first day's lesson, how the space shuttle spins so that the passengers don't have to experience zero gravity.

Flicking on pictures of a shuttle interior, he says, "Look at the walls. They're covered with stick-a-bob, a material that adheres to itself. There are toe and hand locks added to the wall. Each of you will be issued life suits to be put on in case of loss of centrifugal force."

"Oh, oh," someone says—me, I think.

If it had been Emily, she would have said,

> "Oh,
>
> no."

"Don't worry." Buzz smiles at us. "In the ten years that we have been shuttling colonists to the moon, there's been no major problem. This is just a precaution."

As the assistants hand out the life suits, which are also made of stick-a-bob, I wonder what the minor problems were.

As we get into the suits, Buzz explains. "As soon as you are all ready, it's into the simulation chamber."

Emily exclaims,

"With stick-a-bob, we'll all be ready,
It'll hold us to the wall nice and steady."

Salvador Arply butts in with

"If it doesn't, it'll make us very deady."

No one seems to appreciate his joke except Vern, who goes "Are. Are. Are."

Emily calls Salvadore

"A philistine,
Oh, so mean."

Buzz continues. "As soon as the centrifugal force is turned off, zero gravity will occur. When it does, throw yourself against the stick-a-bob wall so that the stick-a-bob jackets stick to it. Get into the toe and hand holds. Remain there until you get used to the sensation."

That should take about fifty years.

My father says, "What if this really happened in space? What good would it do to be stuck to the wall?"

Buzz explains. "That would just be until the backup force is generated. Then the crew, who are issued special suits and have special training, will assist you in getting off the wall."

Off the wall—that's exactly what this whole experience is. I wonder what's happening at the Monolith Mall.

My father nods and then puts his arm around my mother's shoulder.

She puts her arms around his waist.

They've stick-a-bobbed themselves together.

I can't believe it.

As they try to pull apart, you can hear the sound.

Buzz shakes his head. "We'd better rethink these new life suits."

Starr laughs and hugs them both, stick-a-bobbing herself to them.

They're laughing hysterically.

So is April, who joins their group.

Soon everyone else is laughing and joining in, including the Mendez quads, who jump on people's backs.

I watch for a while, not sure of whether I want to be part of it.

If only the Turnips were here.

They're not.

Matthew's not.

I am.

I decide to join the group, careful not to end up sticking to any barfburgers.

Moving is going to take some real getting used to.

13

"This is it." My father places the carryon luggage in the overhead racks.

All around us, people are getting settled into their seats.

Out of the group of one hundred, ten are no longer going.

One woman had claustrophobia and got hysterical when the trainers closed the space shuttle simulator door. The decision was made by all concerned that she would probably have a rough flight and most likely would not do well living in the space shield bubble.

The Smith-Joneses left when they realized that they couldn't convince the officials to break the rules and allow their dog, Puppy-Guppy, to go to the moon because "he's so cute."

Another couple decided to go to London instead, and a third couple decided to divorce.

Three people didn't get past the psychological counselors.

Everyone in my family did.

Amazing.

A voice comes over the p.a. system. "Good morning. This is your captain speaking, Lance Letterman. The crew and I welcome you aboard Orion Flight 114. A nonstop trip, the shuttle will orbit for a day and then we'll take another two to get to our destination."

Three days in space in a closed ship. It's kind of scary to think about. Maybe I'll just pretend that I'm at the Monolith Mall—that's enclosed too. Of course, there, when you step out of the door, there's a sidewalk. And there are a lot of shops to keep you busy. So it's not the same thing. Here there is only one boring "essentials" store. And no sidewalk.

Captain Letterman continues. "Make sure that all of your carryon is safely stowed and that your seat harnesses are securely fastened."

We all do as he says.

The flight attendants move through the cabin, checking on each of us.

The captain's voice comes over the loudspeaker again. "We have a special announcement. Emily Doowinkle will now recite her poem to commemorate the start of the flight."

There's a cough and then Emily recites.

"ODE TO TAKEOFF":

"Sky.

High.

Bye."

Then there's silence.

We hear Captain Letterman say, "That's it?"

"Sure." Her voice is very breathy. "Less is more."

What a flake she is. It's funny to think about a bad poet introduced by some guy named Letterman.

Looking around, I see everyone buckling into the chairs, which look like space eggs. The seats are round and white and padded with Polystyrofoam.

"Push the button marked Close."

I do.

A clear plastic shield closes off the rest of the seat. Now the chair's really shaped like an egg.

I'm in the middle, feeling like I'm the yolk.

"Now," the captain says, "push the button marked Incline."

I do. The space egg and I tip back. It's almost as if I'm in a bed—or a frying pan.

We've rehearsed this procedure a million times, but this one's for real.

The captain's voice booms out. "Flight attendants take your seats."

This is it. There's no backing out now.

"T minus twenty-eight." The captain's voice is now coming through the space egg set.

I think of all I am leaving behind and wonder what I'm heading for.

"T minus fifteen."

I feel so many emotions that I can't sort them out. I can only hold onto my seat and try to stay calm.

Captain Letterman says, "Blast off."

The shuttle does.

Over the sound system, music is playing: oldies like "Off We Go Into the Wild Blue Yonder," the sound track from *2001*, "Lucy in the Sky With Diamonds," "Fly Me to the Moon," and then new music—Rita

Retrograde's first megahit, "Cosmic Cruising," and the Scarabs' latest, "Space Monster Hop."

Space.

It takes only about eighty miles to leave the earth's atmosphere and enter space.

I can't believe it.

From earth to orbit—eight minutes, fifty seconds.

We're going to stay in orbit for one day to see the earth from space, to do some medical experiments, and to launch another communication satellite. Then it's on to the moon.

I really do have trouble believing that this is happening. What's going to happen next?

14 _____

We orbit the earth. There will be twenty-four hours with sixteen sunrises and sixteen sunsets. One sunrise or sunset every forty-five minutes. If I were at Alan Shepard High School right now, that would be the amount of time it takes to sit through a class. It's truly incredible.

Looking out, we see the earth—the land, the seas, the sailing clouds. It's so quiet: no sound of wind or anything.

"Are we there yet?" Starr sits next to me on a couch in the observation room.

I pretend that I don't know her.

She repeats herself. "Are we there yet?"

She thinks she's so cute.

"Go play in traffic," I tell her.

"You want me to go outside and get hit by an asteroid?" She acts hurt.

I nod.

"Play with me, Aurora." She squirms on the sofa. "It's getting boring watching the sun all the time. Can you imagine what it's going to be like on the moon with daytime and nighttime each lasting thirteen and a half days?"

"You're kidding."

She shakes her head. "Didn't you realize that's what happens? Because it takes the moon twenty-seven days to turn once."

"No. I want to be an actress, not a scientist. Why should I know stuff like that?" All of a sudden, it dawns on me. "How do they work it out on the moon? Do we have to go to sleep with the light on for half a month?"

"You always do like to sleep with a night-light, so what's the diff?" Starr grins at me.

"Shh." I punch her lightly on the arm. "Don't say that out loud. What if someone should hear you?"

She just keeps smiling. "That'll teach you to tell me to go play in traffic. If you hadn't daydreamed in class, you would have heard Buzz explain that solar energy is used to power the environmental bubble. Lights can be turned off and on."

"But how can that work during the weeks when it's totally light outside?"

"They use antilights to dim and darken."

"This is too much for me." I shake my head. "Leave me alone with all this scientific stuff. I'm trying to figure out where the Monolith Mall is. That's about as much as I can handle."

She points. "I think it'll be easier to find the Pacific Ocean. Take a look."

All that water. Maybe someone will invent a giant straw that will bring water from the earth to the moon.

Straws. I think of Juna and wonder who she's blowing wrappers at this week . . . how many days of detention she's gotten since I left. She'll probably have so many that by the time she graduates she'll have to go back to after-school detention even though she's in college. . . . I wonder whether Randy's gone out with her yet . . . if she's wearing an article of my clothing to school every day.

The observation room gets boring after a while.

"Exercise time." I get up.

Starr stands up too.

As I walk to the exercise room, Starr follows.

Having a younger sister is like having a shadow.

I wonder if Starr will cast a shadow on the moon.

We pass people who are just hanging out.

Julie Verne is playing old maid with her brother.

April is learning reflexology points from Ellie Malden, a chiropractor.

Emily Doowinkle is agonizing over a poem, trying to find a rhyme for *exhilarating*.

Robert Orsini and Art White, two construction workers, are arm wrestling. Orsini is winning.

The Mendez kids run up to us. Henny grabs one of Starr's legs and Penny grabs the other. Lenny and Kenny grab my legs.

They seem to think we're wishbones.

"Please, please, play Pacfamily with us," they plead.

Starr looks at me. "Want to?"

I think about it. Back on earth, I never would have hung out with little kids. Some of the Turnips used to call them "droolers." Up here it seems like something to do.

I say, "Sure."

We go off to play this biofeedback video game where all the moves are controlled by wiring the person to the machine and having that person use his or her brain waves.

I'm not very good at the game, but neither are the quadruplets, so I don't feel so bad that Starr is terrific at it.

The kids are really fun to be with and they're cute, even if they do wear a person out.

Finally their mother comes by and says, "Nap time."

I think that after being with them I need a nap more than they do but decide instead to go on to the exercise room, where lots of people are working out.

The treadmills are the big excitement. Use it for fifteen minutes at the right time and you get a T-shirt that says, "I jogged America." Use it for ninety minutes and you get one that says, "I ran the world."

I use the treadmill and get my first T-shirt.

Julie and Vern come over as I fall into a chair to relax.

It looks like they took fashion lessons from my parents.

Julie says, "Want to play a game?"

I shake my head. "No thanks. I'm really terrible at games."

Vern sniffles. "They're showing *Rocky 415* in the screening area. Want to see it with us?"

"I've seen it already."

Julie pulls at her limp mousy brown hair.

I wonder if she knows that makeup's been invented. Someone should tell her.

I don't want to hurt their feelings, but they're really not the kind of kids I normally know. They're "Turndowns" instead of "Turnips."

"I have to look for my parents," I tell them.

Starr comes over. "They've reserved one of the private recreation suites for the next couple of hours."

She blushes.

The special recreation suite is the one where people can sign up to go for privacy.

The parents are apparently doing more than medical research.

I wonder if when our parents leave the rooms, they get a T-shirt that says, "I did IT in space."

"So you do have time to spend with us." Julie bites her fingernail. "If you want to."

I don't want to be mean and I don't want to hurt their feelings. I've also run out of excuses. I'll spend time with them, but I hope no one thinks we're friends.

With any luck there'll be some kids on the moon that I can relate to.

With any luck.

15 _____

Gray.

Everything's so gray.

Maybe it's just because we landed during the night.

Maybe it's because everything is really just so gray on the moon.

Last night was weird.

The shuttle slowed down and we all got strapped into our space eggs.

Then we landed.

Everything was quiet.

Someone started to sing, "We're here because we're here because we're here."

Then Captain Letterman got on the loudspeaker and thanked us for flying Orion, said that he hoped we all had a pleasant trip, and told us that Emily Doowinkle had a poem to recite, "Ode to Arrival."

> "Landing.
> Standing."

I giggle.

Someone said that Emily's uncle is a member of

the congressional subcommittee that gives money to the space program.

That explains it.

While we collected our overhead luggage, people in fluorescent space suits helped connect the shuttle door to this large buslike vehicle. It was on stilts with wheels.

When the space shuttle door opened, we all walked through it, right into the bus.

Another vehicle, lower down, was used to pick up and transport all the luggage and equipment.

With everyone on board, the bus slowly moved us toward the city under the bubble—the only one on the whole moon, although there are some shelters built throughout the moon in case the people working in space suits outside of the bubble run into trouble.

Once the bus got there, a tube reached out and connected with it, and we walked through the tube into Luna City. Then we had our new addresses added to the information on our shoulder identidisk.

Luna City . . . my new home.

Starr whispered to me, "I wish I could still goof and say 'Are we there yet?' instead of being here."

I took her hand.

After we got through the passageway, we were immediately taken to the only hotel in town, the Luna Wilshire.

Sleep. . . .

And now it's our first breakfast on the moon, and Lenny Mendez has just hit his sister Henny on the head with a biscuit.

My father looks up from his freeze-dried eggs. "People who live in glass bubbles shouldn't throw scones."

The grown-ups groan.

I'm sitting at the corner of the table with Julie and April.

April is trying to avoid Salvador Arply, who has developed a tremendous crush on her.

He's sitting with Barfburger but staring at our table.

Julie drops some dehydrated egg on her lap.

I ignore it.

She looks at me. "Isn't it scary that we're going to be meeting everyone soon?"

I shrug and act like I'm not worried.

April smiles at her. "I'm a little nervous too. It's exciting though—a new adventure. Just take a deep breath . . . relax . . . and visualize how wonderful it's going to be."

I try but have visions of being surrounded by barfburgers.

Julie chews on the edge of her hair. "It's easy for you two to feel comfortable. . . . I'm starting out in a new place with the same old me . . . and don't tell me the story about the ugly duckling turning into a swan. My parents always try that one on me."

I look at her and think more of a dodo than of a swan but decide to be nice. After all, she is the only person my age that I'll start out knowing at school on the moon.

"I'll help you," April offers. "Positive thinking. I'm sure Aurora will help us do your makeup. And you won't have to worry about what to wear, since there are going to be school uniforms."

I've seen pictures of those uniforms—no one can look good in them.

Maybe Julie will have a chance to start out more even.

April looks at me and smiles.

I nod. "I'll help. It'll be alright."

As I say that to her, I think about how nervous I really am. What if the kids at the school are already in cliques and don't want to add anyone else to their groups.

I always seem more sure of myself than I really am.

"Are you nervous, Aurora?" April asks.

Since there is no one from the old gang around, I decide to be honest. I nod.

"Me too," April says.

Julie makes a face. "I really can't believe that about the two of you."

April speaks quietly. "You have to learn to look closely at people and not judge so quickly."

For a few minutes we sit without saying anything.

I think once more about the old gang and about the old school. Now I understand how rough it is for kids who have to move. I wish I'd been nicer to new kids at Alan Shepard High.

My parents are sitting at the other end of the table having a great time.

Starr is playing with the Mendez quads.

It looks like she doesn't have a worry in the world.

I think about what April said and wonder how Starr really does feel.

Julie says, "Let's make a promise that we'll watch out for each other, help each other out."

I don't know what to say. I really don't like her a lot.

April looks at me. "Aurora, why don't the three of us kind of look out for each other for a while?"

It would make me very happy for April to be looking out for me . . . and for me to be looking out for her. That's what Juna and I used to do for each other. And if Julie's part of the agreement . . . I guess that's just another package deal in my life.

I want April to think I'm a good person, to be my friend, even though she's a couple of years older.

I nod again.

Julie smiles and says, "Friends forever."

"For a while does not mean forever" is what I want to say. Instead I give this little smile which Julie will probably assume means that I agree.

Why am I such a coward?

16

The L.E.B.—Lunar Exploratory Bus—is on its way. We're ready for a tour of the moon after taking our suitcases and stuff to our new home.

Our new home—ha. It's in an apartment complex, the Mayflower. Starr and I have to share a room until more private housing is built.

It's hard to believe that back on earth my parents were really upset about the thought of having to give up our house. Now they say, "This is different. Here we're pioneers."

Parents are just so hard to understand. Julie rushes up. "Sit with me on the tour bus."

"I'm sorry. I've already promised to sit next to Starr." I put my hand on my sister's shoulder.

Julie looks hurt.

"I really am sorry," I say, feeling a little sad that she seems so unhappy . . . but I did promise Starr. . . . And anyway I spent time with Julie on the shuttle.

"Yeah, sure." She walks away and stands by her brother and parents.

"That was kind of mean," Starr whispers. "But I'm glad we're going to sit together."

I realize I've really missed talking to her. "Me too. It's been a long time."

We just stand there for a few minutes.

Starr turns to me. "Aurora, I didn't want to leave either at first. I was just trying to make the best of it."

I look at her.

She's biting her lower lip.

"Why didn't you say anything?"

She shrugs. "They were going no matter what we said. It was no use . . . and you made such a fuss. So I figured I'd be the good kid."

I give her a little punch on the shoulder. "You little creepling. I'm the one who always has to do the fighting."

"You just picked out the lower bunk today." She punches me lightly on the arm. "You big creepling. You wouldn't have gotten it if I fought back."

It's like old times.

I feel better.

The bus pulls up and we get on.

Our parents sit down in the seats in front of us.

They hug each other as if they were still young and not old married people. They are really so embarrassing sometimes.

Tyler, Robert, and Mariana—some of the construction workers—board the bus. Why aren't they immediately starting to build a new home for my family?

April gets on the bus.

She's changed into this great outfit, a pink and gray fluorescent minitoga. On her ears she has flickering-light earrings.

"Sit with me," Salvador Arply calls out and stands up.

She smiles at him but quickly sits down next to Tolin Black, a very cute media guy.

Salvador doesn't look happy, but Tolin does.

April says, "Sorry," but doesn't really sound like she is.

"You'll be sorry," Salvador says. "We could have eventually married and then your name would have been April Arply."

"A hard offer to pass up." April smiles at Salvador for a minute but then turns to Tolin.

Salvador doesn't seem too heartbroken, since he stands up when Emily Doowinkle comes up the aisle. "Care to join me?"

She stares into his braided eyebrows.

"If it's really truly not too much of a fuss.

I'd certainly love to sit next to you on this bus.

I must confess.

The answer's yes."

Why can't she just sit down like a normal person? But I guess you have to be a normal person to sit down like a normal person.

Matthew would really get a kick out of Emily Doowinkle.

I wonder what he's doing right now.

Maybe I don't want to know.

While we were on the space shuttle, it was impossible to have personal mail delivered.

I hope mail arrives soon.

I do want to know what's going on back home.

The Mendez family gets on the bus.

Henny, Penny, Lenny, and Kenny are really hyper.

Mrs. Mendez looks exhausted most of the time.

So does Mr. Mendez.

If I ever have kids, I want them to arrive separately —with a baby-sitter attached.

The driver steps inside, carrying a clipboard. "Hi. Welcome. My name is Ted Cleaver. I'm the tour bus driver . . . and a greenhouse tender . . . and the coroner."

"I bet people are just dying to see him," my father says.

Starr groans. "Dad. Don't be gross."

Ted continues. "We will now begin our tour . . . just to familiarize you with the area. Later you will be able to explore on your own."

The bus moves forward.

"As you know, we have named this part of Luna City 'Da Vinci,' after the artist who envisioned the life of the future. At present, counting all of you, there are seven hundred and fifty people on the moon. Forty-five are children."

"A real small town." My mother grins at my father. "Just what we wanted—the chance to be small-town medical practitioners."

Ted continues. "We all hold many jobs, in our specialties and in other fields. Almost every adult does volunteer work in the schools—teaching, tutoring, and counseling. The students also help out in various areas."

Being a student is going to be my full-time job, I

think—that and being a cheerleader, if they have them.

The bus stops at a five-story building. Ted says, "This is our all-purpose building—government offices, meeting room, the general store, the school, the hospital, the television and movie rooms are all here."

TV and movie rooms—I just realize that there are none in our new home. And *the* general store. Just one store? No Moon Mall? How do they expect me to survive? What do kids do to have fun up here?

"You will notice that this building is covered by a six-foot thickness of lunar dust to protect it against cosmic rays. In the unlikely event that something happens to the glass bubble covering our town, we are all to take shelter in this building."

Oh, great. Damage to the bubble will be something to think about late at night when I'm not dreaming about earth.

He starts the bus up again.

I look around.

The Mendez quads are doing somersaults in the aisle, all except for Lenny, who is busy being bus-sick.

My parents are holding hands.

Tolin and April are laughing at something.

Salvador and Emily look very interested in each other.

Julie is handing Vern a tissue.

What a drip.

I remember our promise and wave to her.

She either doesn't see me or is pretending that she doesn't.

The bus stops in front of two large buildings.

One is the lunar processing plant.

Ted tells us, "Lunar soil is made up of forty percent oxygen, twenty percent silicon and twenty to thirty percent metals. We use this plant to convert the moon's natural resources into necessary things. The dust is used to make concrete. The silicon is made into solar collectors, semiconductors, and glass. The metals, especially the aluminum and titanium, have a variety of uses."

I feel like I'm sitting in science or in one of Buzz's classes. . . . I wonder what he's doing right now. . . . Probably out recruiting the next bunch of suckers to come to the moon.

"Next to this building we have our solar collectors and solar power unit . . . and next to that we have a large antenna for radio astronomy and a telescope. The moon offers the earth a great deal as a research base as well as being the gateway to exploration of other planets."

Ted sounds very proud. I wonder whether I will ever care even half as much about all of this.

Next comes the water processing plant, where a limited amount of water is being taken from the ice transferred from the poles. "We're trying to become absolutely self-sufficient. Until recently we have had to bring water from the earth—an expensive and bulky proposition. Now we have worked it out so that we combine hydrogen brought from the earth with eight times its weight in lunar oxygen and create enough water to sustain life and to bathe twice a week."

"Yeah! Only two times a week." One of the Mendez quads yells.

Aarg. Only twice a week.

I'm going to have to wear a scarf on my head for the other five days. This is so gross. I want to go home. If my parents wanted a land filled with adventure, we could have gone to Disney, the fifty-first state. They don't ration water there and can wash their ears any time they want to.

The bus starts again.

I realize that we are the only vehicle on the road.

"Where are the rest of the cars?" I ask.

Ted smiles. "There are no private vehicles. The only vehicles are for scientific exploration and manufacturing purposes. We do have an ambu-unit to respond to emergencies. It can go on land or air."

No cars. . . . In another two years I was going to be able to get a driver's license and cruise around.

"There's no place to go," Starr says softly.

"I noticed." I want to cry.

We hold each other's hands.

Ted points out the greenhouse. "Here we grow tomatoes, cabbages, carrots, and sweet potatoes."

"Yuck," Henny Mendez says. "I want a hamburger."

Ted smiles again. "We make tofuburgers. There's not enough water yet to sustain livestock. On special occasions, when a ship arrives, we often have a delivery of fresh meat and fish. Otherwise we use a lot of freeze-dried foods."

"Double yuck." Henny makes a face.

"How often do the ships arrive?" Tolin wants to know.

"Every couple of months."

I wonder if you can make french fries out of sweet potatoes. I wonder if Pizza Hut delivers.

Ted explains how the bubble is equipped with switches to turn on light or dark as needed. Also with air conditioning, heating, and a backup generator because of the extremes in temperatures.

The bus passes a group of private houses.

Ted announces. "We started out with prefab structures brought up from earth. Now we are becoming more self sufficient."

As we continue on our drive, Ted talks about the things located outside our bubble—the mass driver, which acts as a lunar electromagnetic catapult to send materials to space; the pipeline that brings in the polar ice; the government surveillance areas.

The final stop on the tour is the historical park, Sea of Tranquillity, where the first people set foot on the moon. There's a plaque about it, with the quote about the small step, and there's another sign:

HOUSTON, TRANQUILLITY BASE HERE
THE EAGLE HAS LANDED

The eagle has landed—that proves it.

This place is for the birds.

17 _____

Dear Juna,
  Could you and the gang organize
a rescue party and ——
        GET ME OUT OF HERE!!!!
    Life on the moon is the pits
(and I don't mean zap pits.)
    While I was supposed to be
using the computer to do a research
paper, I made out a fact sheet for you.
    I'm depending on you for all of
the gossip (*especially* about Matthew.)
    Now about my rescue party—
how about making that *the*
freshman class project ?!?!?
        ♡ ♡ ♡ and XXX,
            Aurora

FACT SHEET

ABOUT SCHOOL

1. This is definitely not Alan Shepard High School.
2. There's only one person in the senior class, Karlena Leibnitz. I bet that there's a short yeardisk at the end of the year.
3. There were only twelve kids total in the four high school grades. Now there are fifteen. Actually, there isn't even a separate high school. All forty kids from first through twelfth grade (nicknamed the Eagles) are in the one large room with portable divider screens, computers, and a library.
4. The very short people running and crawling through our classroom sometimes are the kids from the other room who range in age from babyhood through five and are nicknamed the Eaglettes.
5. There are no cheerleading tryouts. There's no squad. There's not even a team, and if there were, there would not be other high school teams to compete against.

6. Cafeteria food is disgusting. Today for lunch we had mystery dehydrated substance and lumpy mashed sweet potatoes.

7. There is no one here like the kids at Shepard. It's not that they're all barfburgers. It's just that they are different and wouldn't fit in with us. (And I don't really fit in with them. It's so hard. Sometimes I want to tell them that in my old school I was someone . . . so that they know . . . so that I don't feel so all alone. But I don't think that would be a good move.)

8. There's definitely no one here like Matthew.

9. Mr. Wilcox, the teacher, is also the principal, chief guidance counselor, and media special-ist. He's cuter than any teacher at Shepard . . . also nicer. He's got a sense of humor and he actu-ally likes to teach. With his smile and gorgeous blue eyes, Mr. Wilcox could probably have been a video star. To answer the question that I know you'll ask— yes, he's married. . . . To an-swer the question that I know

Cosmosa will ask—no, he doesn't fool around.

10. There is no truant officer at the school because there is no place to go when you cut. (It's kind of hard to think about a senior cut day, with only the one senior, Karlena.)

11. Every student has to do a school service project. Mine is to work with the Eaglettes. They are very short and sticky. Eventually I will have to do a community service project as well.

12. Each new kid is assigned a guide. Mine is this guy named Hal Brenner, but I've never asked him to guide me. He's a real brain, a junior. Tall and skinny, he's funny (funny ha ha, not funny weird). All of the kids here really seem to like and respect him. He's okay, I guess, but I have a feeling that he'd never fit in on earth . . . at least not with our group.

13. Starr's guide is Hal's younger brother, Tucker. I think she has a crush on him.

14. I miss having a best friend.

15. I want to go back to Alan Shepard High School.

ABOUT TOWN

1. Luna City is nothing like our hometown.
2. There's no weather here because there's no atmosphere.
3. There's no atmosphere here (and I'm not talking weather).
4. The general store is definitely not the Monolith Mall. In fact, if it were located there it would go out of business. It's one large room and it specializes in out-of-date merchandise.
5. A lot of time is spent looking at mail order catalog disks. It's not the same thing as being able to try on stuff, and anyway what difference does it make because of the stupid uniforms.
6. There are no pets in town, no cats, no dogs, not even a gerbil. The good news is that you never have to look down at the sidewalk. The bad news is that there's nothing to pat on the head, nothing to lick you and roll over to be tickled (except maybe one of the Eaglettes).
7. There are no launderettes or dry cleaners on the moon. You take

your dirty clothes into an ultrasonic room and the dirt gets
vibrated off. The same procedure
is used to clean human beings.

8. I miss being able to escape into a
   bathroom and relax in a tub for a
   couple of hours. (We're allowed
   only six minutes in the shower,
   two times a week.) Ultrasonic
   cleaning is not warm and comfy.
9. There are no birds here, which
   makes Tranquillity Base Park a
   very clean place. Boring, but
   very clean.
10. I want to go home.

18 _____

"Aurora Borealis Williams, you whine too much," my father says as I get into the dentist chair.

I stare. "What do you expect? You're going to be drilling my tooth."

"What do I expect? What do I expect?" He flings one of his arms up in the air and puts his other hand on his forehead. "I'm a painless dentist who uses the best, newest techniques. What do *you* expect?"

I think that some of my flair for the dramatic may come from him.

He hands me a metal rod which is attached to a box with dials. "Here. Hold this. If it starts hurting, remember to turn the power up. With TENS, you will feel no pain."

TENS—that's Transcutaneous Electrical Nerve Stimulation—current goes through the skin and stops the pain.

It's weird, but it works. I like TENS better than when he uses acupuncture, which also works, but I hate it when he twists the needles.

"Open wide." He looks in to see what's happening.

I am a captive audience.

"Aurora, you've done nothing but complain since we've gotten here. Nothing's good enough for you. Look at how well Starr's adjusting. Why can't you? You're the oldest and should be setting the good example, not Starr."

"Aar iz a grep."

"Starr is not a creep." My father, from all his years of dentisting, is very good at translating from mouths filled with equipment. "She's trying very hard at school, making new friends, and being helpful to her parents. All you do is whine. You hate school . . . you hate the moon."

"I oo ate ih."

"You came up here prepared to hate it. And now all you do is whine."

I hate it when parents get an idea or word in their minds. Then that's all the kid hears. My parents are really into using the word *whine* this week.

I sit still while he's looking into my mouth. "I found the problem. The gemstone we implanted in your tooth to help fix the problem with your knee has to be replaced."

He hums as he fixes it. My father's really into the relationship of teeth to muscles and organs and to the healing power of stones and colors. I hope he stays so involved that he forgets to lecture me anymore.

"All done," he says, taking away the equipment.

I get out of the chair.

"Aurora." He puts his hand on my shoulder. "Your mother and I are really concerned about you . . . and your whining is making our lives miserable.

We're very happy here, except for you. We want you to be happy here—to at least try."

"Whining doesn't make me happy either," I tell him. "I'm really truly honestly miserable. You just don't understand. You never understand."

"I understand that you're not doing anything to *not* be miserable."

I sigh. "Look, Dad. I'm going to need a written excuse to get back into class," I say.

He writes it out. "Think about what I said . . . and I don't want you and Starr fighting anymore."

I'll think about it, but I won't change my mind. And the fight last night was not my fault. It was hers. All I did was put a sign on my body and lie down on the floor. The sign read "Died of mooning around . . . please return to earth."

My parents just pretended I wasn't there.

I added another sign to my body: EARTH RE-ARRANGED SPELLS HEART.

Starr's the one who caused the trouble. She put her foot over me and said, "Let's pretend that Aurora's a grape. I'll step on her and we'll get a little wine. Whine, get it?"

So I bit her toe.

She definitely deserved it.

As I leave my father's office, the mailperson arrives.

"There's a letter here for you."

I grab it out of his hands. "Oh, thank you. Thank you. Thank you."

It's a viddisk from Juna . . . all covered with 3D sticker lips that say SWAK.

I'm so excited. "Dad, can I look at the disk here—use your computer? It'll just take a few minutes."

He shakes his head. "You have school. You'll have a lot of time afterwards to see it."

I can't understand how he can be so mean, but I don't want to make a fuss in front of the mailperson, so I leave quickly.

There are computers at school.

I'll use one of them.

My father can be so insensitive sometimes.

I really don't think he understands what I'm going through.

I can't wait to get to school to see my letter.

19 _____

"Okay, kids, go work at your computers." Mr. Wilcox runs his hand through his blond hair.

We all go quietly to our computers and put on our headsets so that there will be absolute quiet.

What luck. Now I can see the viddisk.

Ms. Feldman, the classroom aide, is absent.

No townspeople were scheduled to teach today.

It's Karlena's turn to help out with the Eaglettes, so I don't have to do it.

Mr. Wilcox has total charge of the whole first through twelfth grade, with only Karlena's help.

He needs a mental health hour.

He deserves one.

It's like back at the old school when a teacher would give a silent study hall. They always acted like it was because the assignment was so important. We, the kids, always knew it was because they'd had enough of us.

At least Mr. Wilcox is honest about it.

I take out the viddisk letter from the gang at the old school and insert it into the computer.

It opens with an entire room filled with the old gang.

They are obviously turning this letter into an occasion for a party—one that I would give anything to be attending.

People are smiling, waving, making devils' horns with their fingers and putting them behind other people's heads.

Juna yells, "A toast for Aurora" and everyone throws toast up in the air. I know that they did it to remind me of all the times we went to see this weird old movie, *Rocky Horror Show*.

The old gang would laugh if they knew that we only had one movie each week up here, which plays once.

Someone yells, "Turnip the music" and the whole gang sings, "For She's a Jolly Good Fellow" to me.

I wish the kids up here could see how much the old gang liked me and how popular I was.

Each person gives me a personal message and then goes into another room for the continuing party.

"We miss you . . . your laugh . . . your fun . . . your neat way of dressing."

It's a good thing that they can't see me now in this disgusto barfburger school uniform.

"Guess what? I made cheerleading," What's-her-face says.

I hope she gets her lips caught in the megaphone.

Brandonetta gets up in front of the camera, wearing dangling earrings that are really minispeakers. She sings, "We miss you, Aurora. Oh, yes, we do."

With her voice, she's either hitting the key of high C or Luna C.

"Don't do anything I wouldn't do." That comes from Alexis, who does everything.

She should come to the moon and have to deal with a place where there are no cars and it's hard to find a place for kids to go for privacy, let alone to find someone you'd want to be with.

A couple of the shyer kids just wave and leave.

Davie Arnold, the class clown, tells three very dumb jokes, including "Why did the chicken cross the universe? . . . Because he was being chased by Pluto."

Ralph Norton oozes onto the screen to ask me if I'd "made it" with any E.T.'s.

Juna comes on, filling me in on all the gossip: who's going out with whom, who's broken up, what's the latest fad.

She's got on one of my T-shirts, the one with hot purple sequins, showing that she's keeping her promise to wear something of mine every day to keep me part of the group.

She shows me how to do the latest dance step, the Quark.

Then she says, "Aurora, you are my best friend. I miss you so much." She starts to cry and hurries off the screen.

Finally, Matthew is in front of the camera.

He looks uncomfortable, like he used to when he had to get up in front of the class in fifth grade and give a report. He looks down at the piece of paper in his hand and says, "I miss you. . . . I got a B average this semester, which isn't bad with all the work I have to do as class president. . . . I'm getting my driver's permit next month. . . . I'm two inches taller. . . . I thought of a new Baskin-Robbins flavor, sweatsocks sherbet. . . . And Aurora, I miss you a whole lot."

He leaves.

I start to cry . . . a whole lot.

I wish he was here to put his arms around me.

I put my arms down on the table and lay my head on them.

I'm so miserable that my whole body hurts.

I don't even care if anyone sees how awful I look when I'm crying.

If the scientists up here could bottle my tears, there would never be a water shortage.

Someone puts his hands on my shoulders and whispers, "Aurora, may I help you?"

It's Hal.

20

"Go to the Conference Room." Mr. Wilcox hands us passes.

"It's okay." Sniffling, I look at him and at Hal. "I feel better now."

Mr. Wilcox smiles. "Good. Go anyway. A change of scenery might do you good. It's been one of those days for a lot of people, me included. In the old days I would have said 'Must be a full moon.' Up here I guess that I've got to say 'Must be a full earth.' "

Full earth. When I look up at it now, it looks like empty earth. It's hard to believe I ever walked there with my friends and that they're still there, and I'm not. I try not to look at earth.

We take the passes and leave his desk. It's so embarrassing that everyone has seen me like this. My crying has started some of the Eaglettes crying.

Everyone's staring.

As we walk past Starr's computer terminal, I can see that she's been writing a letter to Grandma Jennifer and Grandpa Josh.

She looks very concerned.

I try to smile to let her know that I'm semiokay.
Hal and I leave the room.

In the hall I think, What am I doing here? I hardly
know this guy. As my school guide, Hal's always willing to help, but I never ask for anything. I mean, how
much guiding does a person need in a school with
only one room?

In class Hal seems nice. Not the kind of kid who
would be in the group at Shepard, but he's not a total
reject.

I'm just glad to be out of the classroom. We walk
down the hall and Hal opens a door. "Ta da. The
Conference Room."

"This is a supply closet," I say.

He nods. "What gave it away? The paper? The
mouse writers? The ribbons? The cassettes?"

"My superior intellect." I grin at him. "That and
the fact that the sign on the door says 'Supply
Closet.' "

"I love a woman with brains." He grins back. "It's
also the Conference Room. Mr. Wilcox decided that
we all sometimes needed a place outside the classroom, and since there's a room shortage, we've dou-
bled up. Look—in the corner, in the back—table and
chairs."

"The Conference Room." I do a few tap steps and
extend my arm as if I'm introducing it.

"Brains and talent too." Hal smiles, and we walk in
and sit down.

I look around. "No windows."

"No problem." Hal stands up, tacks a stored shade

on the wall, and pulls the string down. "Just pretend there's a window behind it."

I laugh.

It feels good to laugh.

Hal sits down. "I thought you might want someone to talk to."

I realize how much I want to talk to him even though we hardly know each other. There's something really nice about him and he's kind of cute, even though his looks aren't the kind I usually like.

He's got curly brown longish hair and brown eyes, the kind that squint a little when the light hits them. I bet he's one of those people who have permanent contact lenses implanted. You can tell sometimes by the way they blink.

I shrug. "I don't know what to say."

He shrugs back. "And I don't know what to say to get you to say what you want to say."

I say, "It sounds like we should sing a chorus of the unsure person's anthem: "Oh, see, can you say."

We do, making up verses as we go along.

Neither of us has a voice that would make the glee club. Of course at this school there isn't one, so it doesn't much matter.

I finally figure out what's so different about Hal from the gang back home. He'd never hang out at the mall . . . and I don't think he'd really like some of the parties that we have. On a scale of one to ten, the old gang would probably rate him a four.

I think he's at least a five.

Softly he says, "It's hard moving here, isn't it?"

I nod.

He continues. "My family was in the first group of settlers, ten years ago. We call ourselves the Pilgrims II. I was only six, so moving here wasn't so hard. I'm used to the place."

"You're *used* to it?" I whisper. "People get used to it?"

He nods. "Yeah, some people actually love it."

I think of my parents and bet that they will.

"I won't." I look at him. "Do you love it?"

He shakes his head. "Not really. I see all the videos and news of the earth and want to see what it's really like. There have been a lot of improvements here, so it's okay, I guess. There are some things, though, that I want to do that I can't do here."

He thinks for a minute. "I thought that you were going to do the talking. I don't discuss this with anyone."

I smile at him. "I'm glad you're telling me this. It makes me feel like I may even have a friend up here."

"Good," he says. "You know, there are so many things I want to do. I want to learn to drive a car and just go out somewhere for a ride. I want to see a play . . . to live somewhere that isn't under a bubble . . . to feel rain and snow again."

We're both silent for a few minutes. Then I say, "I can't do much about most of that, but I can do something about the play. Someday I'm going to be an actress—a wonderful one, I hope. So let's organize the kids and put on a play. I would love that . . . so much."

"Great." He smiles. "We can do this as our community project. You know everyone is supposed to do one."

I did know but tried to ignore it. Working with the Eaglettes was enough.

"Okay," I say. "I would like to do it. I've got to do something up here before I go off the edge."

"You can't go off the edge. The moon is round."

"Thank you, Christopher Columbus." I smile at him.

He grins back. "Call me Chris. Seriously, Aurora, I'd like to make this my community service project if you're really willing to commit to it. I've been talking to people about wanting to change my project. Working at the store for two years is enough. It's time to do something else. I've just got to know that you mean it. It's going to take a lot of work, isn't it? You're the one who's done it before."

I nod. "It'll be lots of work. I'm not sure how much, since I've mostly just acted in plays. But I'm willing to try."

"Great." He smiles.

I nod again. These plans are happening very quickly.

Hal looks at me. "Aurora, you are so different from anyone I know, from anyone that I've ever met."

I blush.

So does Hal.

I change the subject.

"What do you think we should do? Do you think that many people will try out? I don't think the kids up here are going to be very excited to do something with me."

"I think they will if you stop comparing them with the kids back on earth."

"Do I do that a lot?"

"About every three minutes," he says.

"That bad, huh?"

He nods. "Yes."

"I'm sorry. It's just that I miss them so much. I used to feel like I fit in."

He says, "You could feel that again . . . if you'd give all of us a chance."

I think about that and ask, "How come you want to do this project with me? Is it the play? Or am *I* your project? Have they told you to reform me? Is that what this is all about?"

He doesn't look pleased. "Aurora. You're so paranoid. Why don't you lighten up a little?"

I stare at him. "Promise me you won't be doing this as your school service project—the reform Aurora assignment."

He shakes his head. "No, I won't be doing it as a project. I promise. . . . Listen, if this were an assignment that I was going to be graded on, I wouldn't take it and take a chance on ruining my grade point average."

I don't want him to be angry with me. I'm not sure that I could handle that with the way that I already feel after receiving the vidletter. "Look. . . . Truce. . . . I'm really sorry. It's been a rough day. Please don't be angry."

He smiles at me. "Okay . . . truce. . . . Listen, Aurora . . . I've been bored up here and want to try something new . . . and I think you could be fun to work with. I think . . . Anyway, it's worth trying. So let's get started, make a list. What do you think we'll need?"

I start to name some of the things. "A play . . . actors . . . a director . . . sets . . . costumes . . . props . . . a place to put the play on . . . understudies . . . prompters . . . a set designer . . . set builders . . . Hal, this is going to take a lot of work. In junior high I just acted and didn't have to deal with all of this stuff."

"Want to back out before it's too late?" He puts down the pen. "Once we go in and tell Mr. Wilcox and he says yes and we go to the town council and they agree, we have to do it."

I think about how much work it's going to be—not like it used to be at Alan Shepard High School. But there's not a chance that I'll be able to perform at Shepard. My only chance is at Da Vinci, and it looks like I'm going to have to work to make it happen. I look at Hal and give him my answer.

"It's a deal."

21 _____

Starr flops down on her bed. "How come you're getting all dressed up if this isn't a date?"

I try on my third outfit. "Look. This is *not* a date. Hal and I have to go to the town meeting to present our proposal. Once it's accepted, we'll get money to put on the play and to reserve shuttle space for the supplies that we need."

"If it isn't a date, how come you're putting your makeup on so carefully?" Starr persists. "That's what you always do when you want to flirt and impress boys."

"I do not."

"You do too." Starr shakes her finger at me. "Don't try to pretend it's not true. I'm your sister and I know it's true."

"You're a real pain, do you know that?" I throw a pillow at her. "It's not a date, but you can't tell the difference because you've never been on one."

She ducks. "You're so mean. And I do know that it's true. You know it's true too. We all do. I once heard Mom tell Dad that you were majoring in boys, and he

THIS PLACE HAS NO ATMOSPHERE   103

agreed and said that your minor was being a fluff-brain—that you were really smart but didn't use it."

I debate killing the parents.

Then I debate killing Starr but decide against it. If I murder, I'll go to prison, and being in prison on the moon is redundant.

Ignoring her is the next-best solution.

"Aurora . . . Aurora."

I comb my hair.

Starr continues. "It's mean of you to remind me that I've never been on a date. I'm only eleven—it's not as if I'm a total social reject. . . . Am I?"

I continue to ignore her, so that she feels like a total social reject.

When she starts to cry, though, I feel guilty and hug her. "Don't be silly, Starr. Lots of people are late bloomers . . . and you're too young to even be a late bloomer yet."

"Maybe I'll be a nonbloomer." She sniffles. "Non-bloomers get a lot of fertilizer put on them but nothing happens."

I wipe the tears off her face. "Starr, you've got a lot going for you. You're smart and nice and cute."

"I'm so confused. I don't want Mommy and Daddy to call me a fluffbrain when I decide to like boys, which could happen any minute, and I don't want to stop using my computer."

"It doesn't have to be all or nothing," I say. "You can like computers and boys . . . and lots of other things."

I think about what I've just said and wonder if I've ever really liked doing lots of things besides hanging out with the Turnips and having a boyfriend. It's always been easiest to hang out with kids who just hang out. That way I don't have to think about the stuff that really bugs me . . . like my parents . . . and my feelings . . . and not being so sure of myself really.

Starr says, "It's not fair. Even if I find someone I like, how will I know if he likes me?"

I turn to her. "You've got a crush on someone, don't you?"

She blushes.

"I bet it's Tucker."

Continuing to blush, she says, "Please don't tell Hal that I like his brother."

"I won't. But you have to stop saying that I'm dating Hal. I'm not."

"He's so nice though."

I nod. "He is, but he's not my type. We're just friends."

I finish getting ready.

Starr watches. "Aurora, are you really going to leave in a year?"

I sit back down on the bed. "I think so."

She takes my hand. "Even though we fight sometimes, I don't want you to go."

I smile. "It won't be so bad for you. It'll be like being an only child and getting all the attention."

She shakes her head. "I don't think it's better to get all of the attention than to have a sister to talk to about stuff. Especially up here on the moon."

"You know that in a few years I'd be leaving to go away to college—no matter where we lived."

"It's not the same. You know that. Maybe by the time you get ready for college there will be one up here."

I pretend to hang myself. "Could you imagine? If there were a lunar college up here, the sweatshirts would all say 'Moon U'—and that's what the fraternity guys would probably do."

Starr giggles. "Grossiosity."

The doorbell rings.

"It's Hal," my mother calls out.

Patting Starr on the head, I say, "See you at the meeting. And don't worry. It'll work out alright."

I can't believe that statement just came from my lips. I'm the one who thinks that nothing's going to work out.

As I leave the room, Starr calls out, "Aurora."

I turn around. "Yes?"

She says softly, "Mom went out with Dad, and she's not a fluffbrain."

I laugh. "Going out with each other—and staying together—maybe that makes *both* of them fluffbrains."

22 _____

"Hal's got a girlfriend. Hal's got a girlfriend." His seven-year-old sister Natasha and two of her pals follow behind us, singing.

Hal pretends to ignore them.

So do I, even though it's kind of cute. Because I've had lots of boyfriends I don't embarrass easily . . . even though Hal is really a boy who is a friend, not a boyfriend.

Hal, however, is embarrassed.

His face gets redder and redder.

Finally the trio sings:

> "Hal and Aurora in zero gravity,
> K-I-S-S-I-N-G.
> First comes love,
> Then comes marriage
> Then comes Aurora with a baby carriage."

"That's it," he yells, turning to them. "If you little monsters don't leave us alone, you'll be sorry."

The girls take a step back.

He continues. "Now leave us alone."

Natasha says, "Can't you take a joke? You can be so mean."

The girls rush off.

I put my hand on his arm. "Hal. They're just kids."

He looks at me. "Sometimes I get so sick of being the oldest and having the two youngest follow me around all the time and bug me."

I can understand that. "Don't forget I have a younger sister too."

I think about what I've just said to Hal and realize how that's changing. With the move, Starr and I are becoming closer. I need friends and she's becoming one.

Hal and I walk toward the meeting hall.

"In a way it was nice to see you not being so calm and in control. You always seem that way at school."

He laughs. "Right. That's me . . . the kid with the right answers all the time . . . the one who helps everyone out."

I grin at him. "A knight in shining armor."

"A night in shining *amore*," he says.

I'm not great at foreign languages, but I know that *amore* means love in some language. (I always try to know the important words so that I could get along while traveling. *Love* and *bathroom* are the two words that I think are most important to know. I may be a romantic but I'm also practical.)

I curtsy. "You're a lunar knight on a lunar night."

"At your service." He bows deeply and kneels on one knee, pretending to take off a hat.

"Hold that pose. Don't move for a minute." I look in my bag and pull out a star sticker, which I put on his forehead. "I dub thee Sir Hal, rescuer and protector of fair maidens, as long as they are not your sister and her friends. Arise."

He stands up and looks around.

People are staring at us and smiling.

Hal smiles back at everyone. "Haven't you ever seen a starry knight?" He grabs my hand and says, "Come along, fair damsel. I must rescue you from the dragon."

"But Sir Hal . . . how can you rescue me from the dragon when none appears on yon horizon?"

He continues to hold my hand and rush me along. "I'm rescuing you from draggin' along and being late for the meeting."

"Oh, yeck. That pun is perfectly awful."

He stops and stares at me. "Look. I am not perfect. I make bad puns. Sometimes I even yell at my little sister and brother. I get bad grades in chemistry. My locker at school is messy. I repeat, I am not perfect." He smiles at me. "I am not a knight in shining armor. I am a knight in tarnished armor."

"All you need is a little polish," I inform him. "Stick with me. I can make you shine."

He looks at me shyly. "It's a deal."

I look back at him.

All of a sudden I feel a little shy too.

I'm not sure why.

All I do know is that I'm very glad we're becoming friends.

23

The definition of *lunatic* is "moon struck."

After sitting through the town meeting, I can understand why.

Hal and I sit at the edge of the crowd.

I guess that makes us part of the lunatic fringe.

Emily Doowinkle recites her new poem, "You 'n Verse, As in Universe":

"Poem.
Dome.
Home."

The manager of resources, Marc Boswell, announces that while the generator is being recharged only essential equipment should be used.

I hope they consider blow-dryers essential.

I know I do.

Mr. Conway, the greenhouse tender, is next.

He's also the town grouch.

I think every place must have at least one.

Mr. Conway stands in front of the council.

Tall, skinny, and bald, he shakes his fist. "I want the PortaPotties at the edge of town painted fluorescently so that people can find them in the dark and not use my greenhouse instead."

It's the town's greenhouse, but Mr. Conway never quite accepts that fact.

I would think that he wouldn't mind people using the greenhouse instead of the PortaPotty. On earth that stuff is supposed to help things grow.

"Time's up," the mayor yells.

Hal smiles at me. "Every meeting, Conway makes that proposal and every meeting the mayor calls time. The first suggestion Conway made was to rig the PortaPotty doors so that when you clapped your hands, the doors would open in the dark. He forgot to think about what would happen if someone was already in it.

I laugh.

"Aurora Williams. Hal Brenner." The mayor calls us to the front of the room.

I take a deep breath to try to stop laughing.

It's not easy, because I'm so nervous.

This is not acting. It's real life once more.

Hal goes first.

He explains that we want to put on this classic play, *Our Town,* and that Mr. Wilcox has promised to direct, with April assisting. "Tryouts will be held next week if the project is approved."

He sounds so good, so sure of himself.

I'm glad we remembered to take the star sticker off his forehead before he spoke. I'm not so sure he would have been taken as seriously otherwise.

The town council listens and nods. You can tell they know and like Hal.

One good thing about the moon is that kids are treated better, with more respect. I think that's because with a small population everyone is more important, more useful. It's like *Little House on the Prairie,* only it's *Little Town Under the Bubble.*

"Aurora. You're next."

I step forward, hoping I won't get the giggles.

Mr. Wernik, the mayor, smiles.

Even though I'm nervous, I speak clearly and directly, explaining what supplies and costumes will be needed. Hal and I have worked out costs and square feet of shuttle space needed. It won't be much, since we've chosen a play with very little scenery.

While I'm speaking, one of the Eaglettes comes up and attaches herself to my ankle.

I reach down and pick her up, kiss her on the forehead, and finish the sentence.

Working with and caring about the Eaglettes at school has come in handy: she looks at Mayor Wernik and says, "Daddy, I love Aurora."

Mr. Wernik laughs and says, "My daughter Vanya places an unofficial vote *for* the play. How about the rest of us?"

The council votes.

It's unanimous.

As everyone says yes, there's applause.

I kiss Vanya on the forehead and hand her back to her mother, who has come up to get her.

Hal and I give each other victory signs.

It feels great, like we've really accomplished something. Now if only the play turns out as well—if only I can give a great performance. I've always wanted to play the part of Emily. I'm sure I'll get it. I don't think there's anyone else who cares as much about putting on this play as I do, except maybe Hal, and I don't think he's going to try out for the part I want. Partly because I know he doesn't want to act and partly because he would look lousy in a dress.

The meeting ends.

The party begins.

It's a tradition to socialize after the meeting. Almost the whole town shows up. It is really like during the earth's pioneer times.

Fast music comes over the loudspeakers.

Salvador Arply and Emily Doowinkle are slow-dancing. I think this has turned into a serious romance. I wonder what will happen if they get married and have kids. Would two creative artists have a kid who wanted to program computers?

"Want to dance?" Hal asks.

"Yes."

"I've got to warn you. I've spent the whole week practicing."

"With whom?"

He turns red. "By myself . . . and then my mother walked in, saw me, and helped."

We dance.

He steps on my feet seven and a half times.

He whispers in my ear and steps on my foot again. "This is much more fun than dancing with my mother."

I wonder whether she can still walk.

After the music ends, we walk over to the refreshment table.

Actually, Hal walks and I limp.

We try the candied carrots.

Yeccho.

Some of the kids from school join us.

"I'm so excited," Karlena says. "I'm going to try out for one of the little parts, one of the towns-people."

"Me too," Vern Verne says.

I hadn't noticed any parts for barfburgers in the play.

Julie Verne says, "I'll work on the makeup commit-tee."

I smile. "That's great."

April and I helped her make up during the first week of school and she's gotten really good at it.

"Want some ice cream?" Hal asks.

"We have ice cream? I can't believe it."

"Don't get your hopes up. It's freeze-dried." Hal hands me a bar of it.

It's interesting. Not great, but interesting. For a minute I wonder what Matthew would have named it. I feel a little sad . . . but not as sad as I would have expected.

One of the factory workers, Brendon Brando, comes over. "Do you have to be a student to try out?"

Hal shakes his head. "No. Everyone can."

"Great." Brendon smiles. "See you at tryouts then."

As he leaves, I hear Julie say to Karlena "I hope that he gets a part. I wouldn't mind auditioning to be his girlfriend."

The music starts again.

Hal asks me to dance.

I suggest talking instead.

We discuss all sorts of things.

He's the first boy who I don't feel like I have to put an act on for, be someone I'm not. He's really a different kind of friend.

We laugh as he imitates Mr. Conway yelling about how someone keeps using his little greenhouse as a PortaPotty.

I pretend to be the supply person who gave a report on the shortage of toilet paper and what measures to use not to waste it.

An older couple comes over to us.

Hal smiles.

They look nice and comfy, like they would be happy to hug a kid.

Some people just look like that.

My parents don't.

"Aurora, these are my parents."

I feel a little shy. "Hi. Nice meeting you."

"Hal has told us so much about you," Mr. Brenner says.

Mrs. Brenner nods. "I ask him how school is and all he talks about is you."

"Mom!" Hal blushes.

She continues. "It's nice to know that he's found someone he likes so much, and I know that Mr. Wilcox thinks you are a wonderful addition to the school and getting more helpful every day."

"Mom," Hal says, "you make it sound like you were checking Aurora out."

"I was." She nods. "And I've watched her at community meals. A mother likes to check out her son's first girlfriend."

"We're just friends." Hal's face is very red.

Mr. Brenner says, "I'm sure we'll be seeing a lot of you."

"Aurora"—Mrs. Brenner gives me a kiss on the cheek—"it's very nice meeting you."

After they leave, Hal says, "That was one of the most embarrassing times in my life. . . . Parents!"

"I like them."

"I do too." He nods. "I can't believe they did that to me though."

April comes rushing up to us. "Aurora. Hal. You did such a great job getting the money to put on the play. It'll be such a terrific experience to direct. Tolin said he'd help with the sets."

I smile. "Wonderful."

We've both been so busy with our new lives that we really haven't had any time to spend together.

April goes over to dance with Tolin.

I look around.

Starr is standing at the sidelines alone, watching the dancers.

"Hal, would you do me a favor?"

"Anything." He smiles at me.

"Ask Starr to dance. Please."

He nods and says, "Sure. And you ask Tucker to dance. And when the music stops, we'll make sure that the four of us are near. Tucker would like that."

"Has he said that he likes Starr?"

"I'm sworn to secrecy." Hal grins. "But my plan is one that will surely work."

A little sneaky.

But nice.

I like it.

24 _____

"I hope you get the parts you want," my mother says as Starr and I get ready to leave the house. "Have a great day."

This afternoon my mother is going to perform bionic surgery on a worker who was injured in a mining accident. She's been so busy studying procedures that I'm amazed she remembered that today Mr. Wilcox is putting up the list of people chosen for the play.

My father says, "I wish we could do something special to celebrate tonight, like go out to dinner."

"There are no restaurants here," Starr reminds him.

"I know." He looks sad. "I'm very happy up here . . . but do you know what I miss? . . . Those fast-food places, food in bags that always rip before you even get it home, greaseburgers, soda cups that leak from the plastic tops. Also pizza that the delivery boy has tilted to one side, so that the cheese is all in the corner of the box."

My mother says, "I miss sushi."

"Raw fish, yuckiosity." Starr makes a face. "That's like eating from a goldfish bowl."

My mother continues. "And ice cream places that sell soft custard. And I miss my mother's brownies." She pauses. "And I miss Mom too."

We're all quiet for a few minutes, and then Dad says, "After dinner tonight, let's all go out for a family walk and then I'll bring out a hidden surprise that I've been saving for a special occasion—something Grandma Jennifer sent up on the last shuttle."

"How come I never saw it?" My mother puts her hands on her hips.

He smiles. "She labeled it Dental Supplies and told me to open it when you showed signs of missing her."

"Brownies!" we all yell at once, jumping up and down. "Brownies! Brownies!"

When we finally calm down, my father says, "That's for tonight. But now we all have to go to work and to school."

Starr and I kiss our parents good-bye.

This has been a great way to start our day, I think as we leave for school.

"I thought I was nervous trying out for the play," Starr says. "Waiting to find out who's got which part is even worse."

I smile at her. "Don't worry. I bet you'll get a part."

"That's what I'm nervous about." Starr crosses her eyes. "How did you ever convince me to audition?"

"How was a cinch. I told you that Tucker was trying out too. The reason *why* is that I'm sure you'll get a small part and it'll be fun, something different from working with computers. I helped you prepare for

the audition and I'll help you when you're in the play."

"Sometimes you can be terrific." Starr smiles at me.

I smile back.

We continue to walk along the street. Everything is so drab—gray dust, ugly black buildings. The weather's so nothing. I remember the days on earth where sometimes it would rain, or snow, or be sunny . . . never be quite the same . . . and you could wear different types of clothes depending on the weather.

The only time I get wet unexpectedly on the moon is when one of the Eaglettes drools or does worse.

This town is really boring to look at. None of the buildings is taller than five stories. Most of them are covered with lunar dust. The paths are concrete. Outside of the greenhouse and Tranquillity Park, there are no trees, plants, or flowers.

Once you get out of the center of town, there are the industrial sections. There's no reason to go there unless you're industrial (not necessarily industrious), and even if you do go there's not much to do unless you are a worker.

It's not fair. I know that this place was designed to be a way station to Mars, which is being designed to be a beautiful place to go in the future. But they could have done something to spruce up the moon. I don't think it's fair not to just because it will cost a little bit more of the taxpayer's money and will use some of the energy for "nonessentials." What else are they going to spend the money on? A little more color and style shouldn't cost that much. One nuclear bomb would be much more expensive, and they're always buying a new one of those on earth.

I wish they'd think about those of us who have to live here and aren't industrial. We should have rights too.

It's a good thing we're doing the play up here. That'll lighten things up. It'll definitely turn Bored Way into Broadway.

Starr tugs on my tunic. "Are you nervous?"

"About what?"

"About Mr. Wilcox announcing who has what part."

I think about how he had me read for several parts and how he said "Aurora Williams, I am very impressed."

I smile at Starr. "No. I'm just really excited to be able to be in the play. And I can't wait to be Emily—to play her from teenage to grown-up. It'll be great."

"I hope I'm one of the townspeople who have nothing to say." Starr crosses her fingers.

"You'll do fine." I feel more excited than I have since we got here.

As we walk into the classroom, there's a crowd of people around the bulletin board.

"Congratulations on getting a major role," one of the kids says to me.

I grab Starr's hand and rush up to the bulletin board to check out the results.

Barfburger's standing in front of the board.

"Excuse me." I tap him on the shoulder.

He smiles at me and moves away.

I look at the cast list.
Karlena's Emily.
I'm Mrs. Gibbs.
Barfburger is Dr. Gibbs.
I wish I were dead.
Life just isn't fair.

25 _____

I will not let anyone see me cry.

I will not let my tears go any further than the corners of my eyes.

"Oh, no." Starr says. "I have a real part. I'm Rebecca Gibbs."

Great. My little sister will be playing my daughter. Mr. Wilcox must have decided that it was all relative who got which parts.

Mr. Wilcox must have lost his sanity.

Karlena doesn't even want to be an actress. When she graduates, she just wants to get married to her boyfriend, Kael, and live happily ever after.

I don't understand Mr. Wilcox.

Where's Hal when I need him? He's being interviewed and tested by the space psychologists.

"Excuse me," I say. "See you all in class. I've got to go somewhere."

I turn and start walking away.

"Where are you going?" Starr asks. I just walk away.

Mr. Wilcox arrives and announces that school is about to begin.

I continue to walk to the door.

"Aurora," Mr. Wilcox calls out, "I'd like to speak to you."

"Later," I say as I walk out. "I forgot something at home."

There's no way that I'm going to stop until I get out of this building.

"Ten minutes, Aurora," Mr. Wilcox yells. "Be back by then."

I look at my watch, even though I don't plan to be back in ten minutes—or ten hours—or ten days—or ten months—or ten years.

Who does he think he is? He can't boss me around. I won't even be in his stupid play.

Why did he say he was so impressed with my acting ability and then not give me the lead?

I slam the door as I leave the building.

As soon as I walk out the door, I stop.

There's no place to go.

I can't go home.

I want to go shopping—to buy myself something nice to make up for what I'm feeling. Grandma Jennifer would say that's not the right way to handle my problems, but who cares? Anyway, once more, it makes no difference what I want. There's nothing to buy anyway, and if I go to the general store, they'll ask why I'm not in school.

On the moon it's like everyone is a truant officer.

This is a small town and everyone knows everyone else's business. There's not even another town where I can go to escape.

To leave the bubble, I'd have to get a space suit. I

can just see me walking up to the Bureau of Space Suits or whatever it's called and saying "Hi. I'm in a really lousy mood. How about letting me suit up and go for a little walk in the dust?"

Maybe I should just try to sneak out of the bubble without a suit and fry or freeze to death.

I should just quit the stupid play and forget about it.

I did promise to see this through. But that promise was made when I thought that I was going to play Emily.

Aaarg. I just don't understand how Mr. Wilcox could do this to me.

I wish I could go over to my grandparents' house and talk to them while Grandma Jennifer makes brownies.

There is no place to go.

No place but back to school.

I'm just going to have to deal with this myself.

Mr. Wilcox, watch out! Here I come!

26

Mr. Wilcox, watch out! Here I come!

I keep saying that to myself as I stand outside the door, but it's going to be very hard to walk into the classroom.

Everyone's going to be staring at me.

I don't even know if I can talk to Mr. Wilcox without crying.

It's not just that my feelings are hurt. It's also that I'm angry, and when I'm angry I cry.

I was really counting on the play to help me feel better about having to be on the moon, and now it's just another thing that makes me feel terrible.

I open the door a little.

The older kids are working at their computer terminals and Starr is reading to the little kids.

She's doing my job. It's my turn to work with the Eaglettes today. I was so upset that I forgot, and being with the kids is something that I'm really beginning to like doing.

Back on earth it would have been so "toady" to be with little kids. Up here it's not. I'm glad, because I really like working with the Eaglettes. At this moment I'm glad there's something that I still like.

I'm not sure how to handle this—whether to march up to Mr. Wilcox immediately, or do my job and talk to him later.

In some ways I'd love to get all this over with, to let Mr. Wilcox know how I feel, but it's not fair to Starr to let her do my job. It's not easy making the right decision. I'm not even sure there is one right or one wrong decision in all this.

Mr. Wilcox is at his desk holding an individualized writing conference with Vern—barfburger and my play husband.

I refuse to embarrass myself and make a scene.

I'll do my job and speak to Mr. Wilcox when he's alone.

It's so hard to be grown up when all I really want to do is stamp my feet, scream, and throw a temper tantrum.

Walking into the classroom, I concentrate on looking straight ahead at the corner where Starr and the Eaglettes are sitting.

Once I get there I sit down on the floor as Starr continues to read the story. She takes a second to look up, smile, and wink at me.

One of the kids, Dani, kisses me on the knee and then puts her head down on my leg.

Another, Marilla, climbs onto my lap and hugs me.

Putting my arms around her, I kiss her on the forehead.

Starr continues to read, and Marilla sucks her thumb and pats my cheek.

I feel a weird combination of calm and crazed.

Starr finishes the story and I sneak a peek over at Mr. Wilcox's desk. He's meeting with another student.

The Eaglettes, Starr, and I start to build a robot out of Legos and Silly Putty.

I've finally started to relax when I feel a tap on my shoulder.

It's Mr. Wilcox.

It's time to deal with everything.

Watch out, I think. *Watch out!*

I'm not sure whether the warning is for him or for me.

27 _____

"Okay, kids. I'll be standing outside the door. No funny business," Mr. Wilcox calls out. "I don't want anyone to feed a peanut butter sandwich to the computer disk drive . . . or to put a carrot stick into the pencil sharpener to make cole slaw . . . or to tap-dance on each others' heads."

Everyone laughs. Everyone except me.

I hate it when teachers act funny and nice when I'm angry at them. It's always better when everyone hates the teacher. Then I don't feel so alone if I do.

Even Starr laughed.

I almost smiled but then remembered what he'd done to me.

Let Karlena laugh at his jokes.

"Okay, Aurora. Let's go outside." Mr. Wilcox looks down at me.

We stand in the hallway outside the classroom.

I have my arms folded in front of me.

He leans against the wall. "So, Aurora. Do you want to talk about what's bothering you?"

I take a deep breath and nod.

Mr. Wilcox says, "Don't worry. We'll work this out."

I glare. "Don't worry! How are we going to work this out? What you did was so unfair."

"Aurora, tell me exactly what's bothering you."

This is so frustrating. He knows what's bothering me.

Mr. Wilcox waits.

I try to organize my thoughts and then begin. "You know I want to be Emily, and I think I should be. I'm the one who suggested doing the play, and Hal and I went to the council and got permission and support to do it. Also, you said I read really well for the part and you know that I want to be an actress and I have more acting experience than anyone else on the moon. I don't see how you can be so mean and so unfair to give the starring female role to Karlena." I stare up at him.

He returns my stare. "Aurora. You went to the council to get permission to put on the best play possible. You weren't given that go-ahead just so that you could have what you think of as the starring role. And Emily isn't the only major part. There are several, and Mrs. Gibbs is one of them. Karlena, without acting experience, is a lot like Emily. She's grown up here in a small town and she wants a lot of the same things. In that way, the part is easier for her. When Emily dies ten years later, Karlena can handle that scene too . . . with some coaching from you."

Coaching from me! How unfair can he get? Who does he think I am, St. Aurora?

He continues. "The part of Mrs. Gibbs was given to

you because it's very important to the play and it will be a 'stretch' for you. It will help you grow and try out new things."

"But I know that I can be great as Emily."

He smiles at me. "You can also be great as Mrs. Gibbs. You'll just have to work harder."

"Why do I have to try out another new thing? Isn't it enough that I've had to move, to leave everyone and everything I cared about?" I start to cry. "Life isn't fair."

He waits for me to stop crying.

I keep crying because I feel like it and because I figure that maybe he'll change his mind and give me the part of Emily if I keep crying.

No such luck.

Finally I get my crying down to a sniffle.

"Trust me," he says. "By the end of the play you'll see that the right decision was made."

I give him my wide-eyed look. "Please."

He shakes his head. "Aurora. People used to think that the earth was the center of everything and the sun revolved around it."

Why am I getting a science lesson right now?

Mr. Wilcox continues. "Eventually people discovered that earth wasn't the center . . . just as we as people have to learn that we're not always the center, that we're a part of the universe."

"You're telling me that you're not going to let me be Emily."

He nods. "Yes. I'm also telling you something that took me a long time to deal with—that takes most of us a long time to learn."

I sigh. "And Barfburger—I mean Vern—is going to be my husband?"

He nods.

"You sure don't make anything easy, do you?"

"Aurora." He looks at me. "You made a commitment. Now how are you going to handle it?"

I think.

I think about how I promised to work on the play. I think about how hard it's going to be to do the role of Mrs. Gibbs and to be married to Vern, El Barfo. I think about how boring and awful it would be to not be in the play. I think about how I wish the sun did revolve around the earth, to prove Mr. Wilcox wrong. I think about the chance to act again.

"Just call me Mrs. Gibbs."

28 _____

"Did you hear?" Karlena flops down on the couch. "There's a rumor that Rita Retrograde may bring her tour up here."

Rita Retrograde up here—that would truly be lunar rock.

Wait till Juna hears. She's going to be so crazed—this is one concert that not even her parents will lay out the bucks for her to attend. It would be so great if Juna could come up here for the concert and a visit, but that's impossible. Too expensive, everyone will say . . . and a waste of valuable shuttle space.

How can it be a waste to let someone see a best friend, someone like me who can be sitting someplace and all of a sudden, out of nowhere, starts thinking about earth and wonder what's happening there . . . someone like me who sometimes, late at night, kisses her pillow and pretends that it's Matthew even though we haven't been in touch for awhile. . . . Someone like me, who once in a while thinks that she hears her grandmother calling "Aurora"? Seeing my best friend would definitely not be a waste, not to me.

I look at the group of moon kids. They really are nice. In fact, sometimes they're so nice it's almost boring. Cosmosa would never do well up here. The moon therapists would definitely have their work cut out for them if they had to deal with her. Anyway, she's certainly not someone that I miss, but I do miss Juna. Even though I am really beginning to like some of the kids up here, none of them is a best friend the way that she was—is. Juna's the only person who knows my deepest darkest secrets. . . . And I know hers.

Once, for example, when we were about eight years old, we looked at all the people who collected stickers, stamps, and stuff, and decided to have the most unusual secret collections in the world. For two years Juna collected her belly button lint and I collected my earwax. It was so gross, with dust collecting on the earwax ball. At least with Juna's collection, you couldn't tell dust from lint. Finally, Asimov, her dog, ate both of our collections. Only best friends could know about things like that and still be best friends.

As I look around the room, I'm glad, though, that no one up here knows about that grossness. I do wonder what Juna is doing right now and if maybe she's even thinking about me at the same time that I'm thinking about her.

Karlena offers more information. "I also hear that the Plaques are the backup group."

"The Plaques are my father's favorite group," Starr informs everyone. "What else can you expect from a dentist?"

I shrug. He just loves it when they pretend that their guitar strings are dental floss.

Vern comes into the room with two large bowls of popcorn, which he passes around.

I look up at him.

Living on the moon agrees with him. His complexion has really cleared up. My mother says that's because the food allergies aren't so severe up here, since there's not much junk food. Anyway, he looks practically human, but he still laughs like a seal.

It's break time during the play rehearsal.

We really need one.

I'm lying down on the floor, relaxing.

Starr comes up, stands over me, and starts dropping popcorn on my face.

I debate yelling at her but decide instead to try to catch it as it comes down.

"Two points," Hal calls out as one goes into my mouth.

"All right," Tucker yells. "Starr, go for a dunk shot."

Starr gets another two points.

I reach up with my foot and try to get the popcorn to fall out of her hand.

"Penalty," Hal calls out. "Starr gets two free throws."

"That looks like fun," Kael says. "Let's all try it."

We make up the rules. Twenty pieces of popcorn to each player. Two points for each one that goes into the mouth. The person catching the popcorn is allowed to eat each piece once it's in the mouth rather than holding on to it until all twenty attempts are made.

Hal says, "Wait a minute. Shorter people have the advantage. They're closer to the person on the floor."

"But your arms are longer," Tucker reminds him.

"Are. Are. Are." Vern thinks the whole thing is hysterical.

So does everyone else as we break up into teams and play.

Hal's my partner.

Our team gets a total of nine. I catch four and Hal catches five. We tie for the win, sort of. Brendon and Julie claim they've won with nine and a half, since she started to laugh and closed her mouth before the kernel was totally in her mouth.

Somehow, that's not fair. We should at least have a play-off.

"That was a very *corny* game. Are. Are. Are." Vern is having the best time.

Everyone turns on him, pelting him with popcorn.

Mr. Wilcox walks in.

We pelt him.

He pelts back.

Soon everyone is laughing hysterically.

Finally Mr. Wilcox says, "Okay, gang. Back to rehearsal."

I love the play rehearsals.

They're the best ever and I'm really beginning to like these kids a lot more.

I just wish that we could all be transplanted to earth, since there is so much more to do there. I mean stuff like plays and museums and different places to visit. It would be so wonderful to do those things with most of the kids in this group and with some of the Turnips, even though I'm not sure both groups would really understand each other.

Since there's not much chance of our being earth-transplanted, I concentrate on what's happening on the moon.

Right now the play is the major thing in a lot of our lives.

I don't want to think about what it will be like when the play is over.

29 _____

Karlena's rehearsing her scene with Kael, who is playing George, her boyfriend and my son.

I really do have to admit she's gotten really good at the part of Emily.

One of the reasons I have to admit it is that Mr. Wilcox is always saying to me, "Isn't she doing well, Aurora? Aren't you enjoying that scene with her?"

The other reason is that she really does get better every day.

It also helps that Mr. Wilcox keeps telling me how terrifically I'm doing. That makes me work even harder to get better.

To be honest, though, it still does hurt my heart a little to hear Karlena rehearse as Emily.

I try to imagine a tornado breaking a hole in the glass bubble and carrying Karlena outside without a space suit. She would then turn into a freezepop or blobmelt.

Then I would graciously take over her part.

Of course, since there is no weather on the moon, it's not likely to happen.

"Not nice thoughts," Hal whispers, coming up beside me and putting his arm around my shoulder.

Hal's been taking a correspondence course in ESP, doing biofeedback, and generally developing his psychic powers. It's kind of fun for me to watch him and my mother try to talk to each other. However, I'm not sure I like it that he can read my mind so easily.

Starr says it's easier because I'm so much more open now . . . that it's not such a bad thing to be vulnerable like that . . . that she bets I'll be good at ESP someday too.

I think that'll be something to explore when the play's over. Instead of outer space, inner space. There certainly isn't much else to explore on the moon unless you're a scientist.

I put my arm around Hal's waist and we just stand there watching for a few minutes.

Even though Hal and I are just friends, it's nice to be able to hug each other.

I wonder: If someone doesn't kiss and make out during their teenage years, will that person's body rust?

Mr. Wilcox calls out. "Emily. George. Good work. Now I want all actors to try on their costumes, which have just arrived on the space shuttle. Males to the recreation room. Females to the film room. And hurry up. The council is going to need the community rooms in about an hour."

Space is a real problem in space.

"See you later," Hal says to me as he walks away. "Try not to worry about rusting."

I am tempted to remind him that he hasn't had a girlfriend since the fifth grade when he and Karlena, a sixth grader, swore undying love and then she started to grow up faster than he did. I decide not to. He confided that information to me one day when we were having a real heart-to-heart talk and I'd never use it against him. However, this better not be the start of rust references.

Actually I am worrying about things a lot less, including rusting and worrying so much about what people think. It's different up here. Maybe when you live in a place with lighter gravity, people take things less seriously.

A lot of things are getting easier, even at home. My mother's been helping Starr to learn her lines, and my father's going to help with the ticket sales. (The profits will be sent back down to earth to an organization that helps the homeless and hungry. On the moon that's no problem.)

At the apartment we ration Grandma Jennifer's brownies, everyone having a little piece each day. We're down to crumbs practically, but it's like having a link with those we love on earth. Earth—it seems so far away.

I head to the costume room. It's chaos, absolute chaos.

That's probably because Emily Doowinkle is in charge of costumes.

She hands me a garment bag.

"Mrs. Gibbs, here's your dress.
Take care of it. Don't make a mess.
It's a little out of date, I do confess."

I look at Julie, who grins at me and whispers, "I wish she'd rhyme a little less."

We giggle some more and I put on my outfit with Julie's help.

Julie says, "When we came up here on the space shuttle, I never really thought we'd be doing things together and that I'd be having a great time with you."

I nod. "Me too, and I really appreciate the help you've given me with the costumes."

She blushes. "Thanks. I want to let you know how much I appreciate the way you and April helped me with makeup and stuff in the beginning."

"Even though we haven't been close since then?" I mention a truth that makes me feel guilty.

She helps me put on the rest of my costume. "Yes, because it made me feel more comfortable to be around other people. And now Karlena and I are good friends. Did you know that she's asked me to be bridesmaid at her wedding?"

"No, I didn't know. Terrific!"

It's weird. I'm happy for Julie. Also, I'm a little jealous that they like each other more than they like me.

"I guess things have changed a lot for both of us since that shuttle ride," Julie continues. "We're both much happier now."

"I guess we are," I say softly. "I guess I am."

We smile at each other.

Starr comes over and stares at me. "What an outfit."

I look in the mirror. I can't believe I'm wearing

stockings with seams (they probably never even heard of stocking spray) . . . funny-looking shoes . . . a dress like the early 1900s. It's so weird to be in clothes that are like the ones worn over a century and a half ago.

I'm surprised that any female wearing an outfit like this would ever show her face . . . but actually that's about all she ever could show. Everything else was covered.

Starr shows me how she looks in her outfit. "Ugly-osity."

People are all giggling and pointing at one another.

"I wonder how all the people in *Our Town* would do in Luna City," Starr says as she takes the bow out of her hair and puts it on her upper lip, pretending it's a mustache.

Karlena thinks about it for a minute. "Actually, I bet they would do okay once you put them in our clothes."

"I guess some things never change," I say. "I bet even Cleopatra worried about pimples. Kids have always had problems with their parents—and brothers and sisters. Look at Cain and Abel."

Karlena grins. "I'll remind my parents of them when they complain about my sister and me fighting."

Emily Doowinkle calls out.
                "No vacations.
                Time for alterations."

While people go off to get their costumes fixed, I

think about the play and about how good it's going to be.

I kind of wish that Juna and Matthew and the rest of the Turnips could see me in it.

Some of them would be more interested in the cast party than the play, but some of them would really like *Our Town*.

If only Grandma Jennifer and Grandpa Josh could be at the performance.

We'll send them a holovideo, but it won't be the same.

I know they'll love the play, and Starr and me in it.

I sure do miss them.

In Grandma's last letter, she said they're taking courses at the local community college. Grandpa's getting his brown belt in karate and she's getting her brownie belt in baking.

30

Dear Grandma Jennifer and Grandpa Josh,

Thanks sooooooooooooooooooooooooooooo much for sending up more brownies. We really needed a new supply. When it got to the point where there were only crumbs left, each of us would lick our thumb and press it to the bottom of the box. The thumb owner could then eat whatever crumbs stuck to the thumb. It was not only gross but a little unfair: Dad's got the biggest thumb so he got more than anyone else. He said that was okay because he's the family breadwinner. Mom said, "Wait a minute. I'm also the breadwinner. With your big thumb you are the brownie winner."

So I want you to know that the new shipment arrived in the nick of time and is truly appreciated. Next time do you think that you could also send up the unwashed mixing bowl and spoon?

You asked how I'm doing up here.

Who knows?

It's hard to explain to you since I'm not so sure myself.

In the last mail delivery there was a vidletter from the Turnips. They had just wrapped the vice-principal's house totally in toilet paper and were at Juna's to celebrate.

It was good to see them, but I felt a little strange.

There's a new girl in the group. She says her nickname is "Tapioca . . . because I'm so sweet," giggle giggle. She was hanging all over Matthew, who didn't seem to mind—not one bit. Now I know why he hasn't written lately. I've always disliked tapioca pudding because of the lumps. Maybe that's how Tapioca got her name—because she is such a lump, giggle giggle.

Juna filled me in on all the gossip. You probably know most of it, though, since she also said that she went over to your house for a visit. You're all so lucky to be able to see each other in person.

Anyway, in case you haven't heard, here's the news.

One day, Brandonetta took off her Walkperson earrings and started listening to everyone. A week later she left the Turnips and started hanging out with other kids.

Randy finally asked Juna out. The detention monitor gave them time off for good behavior. She said she's so happy, it feels like she's walking on air. He's probably using his telekinetic powers on her.

The Turnips, on the vidletter, had comments about the kids on the moon. (I had sent them a picture when I got here and must confess that I wasn't very nice in my descriptions of some of the kids. But that didn't give the Turnips the right to be so cruel.)

They said that Vern was more than a barfburger. (I don't call him that anymore, even though he's still far from perfect.) Anyway, they said that when Vern arrived on the moon, "the eagle has landed" should have been changed to "the ugle has landed."

I'm not sure I would fit in with the Turnips now.

Sometimes I wonder what all the Turnips feel inside, what they would be like if they had to leave the group and go somewhere else. I know I've had to change a lot.

I also wonder what the moon kids would go through if they had to move.

The parents are pretty much the same, only we're getting along a little better.

Mom just did the first combination heart, lung, and liver bionitransplant on the moon and Dad's doing all sorts of experiments with herbs, essence-of-flower remedies, and use of visualization techniques to straighten teeth, instead of using braces. *(So far the visualization hasn't worked so he's going to try post-hypnotic suggestion next.)*

They've joined a bridge club. (Dad says that dentists use bridge clubs on the heads of people who never remember to floss. That's what Dad calls "a little dental humor." None of the rest of us thought it was that funny, probably because we're not dentists.)

Dad's also on a team in the lighter-than-air hockey league. They play in an area with reduced gravity. Everyone weighs less, including the players. Dad likes that a lot because he's put on about ten pounds since he's gotten here. Dehydrated food seems to agree with him . . . or maybe it was the extra brownie crumbs.

As for Hal, I think I really like him a lot. It's so weird though. He's not like any other boy that I've liked before or thought I would like. It's scary that my feelings could be so strong if I'd let them be. He's so different from all the other guys I've dated. I don't want to talk about this anymore. It makes me too nervous to feel so close to him.

I'm not sure of a lot of things.

It sure is hard growing up.

It sure was hard being a kid.

Is it going to be hard being a grown-up? (Don't tell me. I don't think I want to know the answer.)

I really wish you could be here to see the play. It's going to be terrific.

To answer your other question: I don't know anymore whether I'm going to leave at the end of the year or not. I'm not sure where I belong anymore. It's another thing that I don't want to think about right now.

What I do want to think about is how much I love you both.

Miss you,

Aurora

♡♡♡♡♡♡♡ and XXXXXXX

31

"Break a leg!" Tolin sticks his head into the green room and smiles at the cast before going back to the prop room.

"How come he said that?" Karlena asks. "I thought he liked us."

"It's an old theater tradition," I tell her.

"Break an ankle!" Someone yells out.

"A fingernail!"

"A toenail!"

"An armpit!"

"A pimple!"

"That's gross!"

"Break a gross!"

The cast is definitely getting hysterical.

The play begins in less than an hour.

It's our first performance.

Tomorrow we do a matinee, so that the little kids can see it without staying up too late, and then we have a final performance tomorrow night. That way, everyone on the moon who wants to can see the play.

I look around the room.

Tucker and Starr are going over their lines again and again.

She's biting her fingernails so much that soon she'll have to start on Tucker's fingernails.

Karlena is looking very nervous, taking in little gulps of air.

Kael brings her a glass of water, and then they kiss for a very long time.

I'm surprised that she can breathe at all after that.

Watching them makes me feel lonely.

People are pacing around the room.

I sit in my chair, trying to be calm and centered. It's not easy.

Vern walks in and says, "There are eighty billion people out there."

Either he's exaggerating or a lot of aliens from other planets have just rocketed in for their first Off-Off-Off-Off-Off-Off-Off-Broadway play.

Hal comes over and kneels down in front of me. "Do you want company or do you want to be alone? Since I'm already in this position, would you like me to propose to you?"

I look at him. "Just hold my hand for a minute."

He does, and it helps calm me down.

"Thanks." I smile at him. "And how are you doing?"

"Fine, since I don't have to act. Aurora, about the cast party tomorrow night: I know we'll both be there, but do you want to go as my date?"

I think about it for a minute.

He starts to joke. "If you don't want to go as my date, you can go as my fig . . . or as my raisin. I mean, after the play you won't be Mrs. Gibbs anymore, so going out with me wouldn't be bigamy or whatever it's called." He's definitely not in practice asking for a date. "Or we could go separately. Listen, maybe this wasn't the right time to ask you."

I look at him and smile. "Yes. I'd love to be your date. It gives me a raisin to really look forward to the cast party. Then the thought of having a great time won't be a *fig*ment of my imagination."

He groans at my puns and grins at the same time.

Mr. Wilcox arrives. "Please. Everyone out but my actors."

Hal kisses my cheek. "See you later."

Everyone but the cast leaves, and Mr. Wilcox looks at us. "All right. In just a few minutes, you'll be having a great time."

"Why? Did someone call off the play?" Tucker asks.

There's nervous laughter.

Mr. Wilcox says softly, "You've done the hardest work already. Now I want you to take a deep breath and get into character."

Inhaling deeply, I try to get centered.

I become Mrs. Gibbs. I think about waiting for my husband, Dr. Gibbs, who has gone out to deliver a baby. I think about having to wake my two kids up soon and about preparing breakfast for everyone.

I think about being in 1901, not 2057.

"Take your places," Mr. Wilcox calls out. "And don't look at the audience."

We take our places.

I try not to look at the audience.

Our Town begins.

32 _____

The audience applauds like crazy for the second night in a row. We are a hit! There are six curtain calls. Everyone thinks we're great.

Mr. Wilcox was right, even though I hate to admit it. Mrs. Gibbs was the right part for me.

After the last curtain call, Kael steps forward to speak for the cast and crew. "We want to thank Mr. Wilcox and April Brown for all their help in putting this play on and want to give them a token of our appreciation."

Hal comes on stage, carrying a director's chair with Mr. Wilcox's name printed on it in moon-day-glow colors.

Starr hands April a neon necklace with a silvery moon part and a red sparkling heart.

Everyone in the cast and crew chipped in. We had the presents sent up on the space shuttle.

April looks happy and says, "Thanks. This has really been one of the best experiences of my life."

The audience applauds and cheers April, and Tolin whistles loudly.

It's Mr. Wilcox's turn next.

He talks about how proud he is of everyone. Then he says, "I want to take this opportunity to especially thank the two young people who had the idea, got the funds, and have worked very hard in different areas to make this production a success. Let's have a special hand for Hal Brenner and Aurora Williams."

Hal and I look at each other.

He takes my hand in his and says, "This really is a very special hand."

We step forward and there's a lot of applause.

I'm so happy and proud.

Mr. Wilcox says, "I'm probably crazy to let myself in for all this work again, but I can't let the director's chair go to waste. So let's start an official acting company and put on more productions."

The crowd goes wild.

So do the cast and crew. We hug and kiss each other as the audience begins to leave.

Then it's all over. All those months of work, and in two days it's over.

I feel a little empty.

"Cast party," Mr. Wilcox calls out. "Strike the set. Get out of costume and be in the rec room in twenty minutes."

We take the set down and apart. Soon there is no more Grover's Corners and *Our Town*. It's back to the twenty-first century and "Our Moon."

Heading to the costume room, Karlena and I smile at each other.

"You were great," I say, meaning it.

"You too." She hugs me. "Thanks for all the help. I'm so glad that we've become friends."

"Me too." If I were back on earth, I think that I'd be homesick for her and the other kids on the moon. I wish that it was the future and that someone had invented a way to be in two places at the same time.

Starr comes running up. "Firstly, I want to know when we begin the next play, and twoly, I want to know if you think I'm good enough to get a part in it."

"I don't know when we start, but I do know that you're getting better. It'll just depend on what the play is," I tell her. "And Starr, *twoly* is not a word and I'm not sure that *firstly* is either."

"Now it is," she says, and begins to sing "I love you twoly."

Being in the play has definitely gone to Starr's brain.

We go to the costume room and change.

Emily Doowinkle recites:

> "Play.
> Day.
> Cast.
> Last."

I wish we'd taken up a collection to send her to poetry school.

When I go back to the stage area, Mr. Wilcox and Hal are talking.

As I join them, Hal hands me a rose.

"Thanks," I say. "I bet this cost you a whole month's allowance."

He shakes his head. "I promised Mr. Conway I would help him to fertilize the greenhouse."

I cross my eyes and ask, "How?"

He grins. "We're using *chemical* fertilizers, silly."

Mr. Wilcox changes the subject. "Aurora, before the cast party starts, I want you to know that I think that you've grown tremendously, and not just as an actress."

"Thanks," I say softly, knowing what he means.

He continues. "You've also done a great job at school with the Eaglettes. They really love you."

"I love them too." I smile.

"That makes me want to be an Eaglette again," Hal says.

"All this praise makes me sound like a Goody Two-shoes," I tell them.

Both of them say "NO!"

Mr. Wilcox says, "Maybe when you stop mentioning earth every five minutes."

"She used to say it every three minutes, so she's improving," Hal says. "What drives me nuts is hearing the name Matthew uttered constantly."

I ask, "What if I say 'ER THanks for the compliment, but I need assistance with MATH. YOU will help me, won't you?' Is that allowed?"

"She said MATH YOU again." Hal slaps his hand on his forehead.

Mr. Wilcox shakes his head. "And ER THe. I guess she's not quite turned into Ms. Two-shoes yet."

Mr. Wilcox leaves us and Hal touches my hair. I kiss him on the cheek.

"I thought this was a date," he says.

I kiss him on the lips.

"That's more like it," he says, when we stop to breathe.

We kiss again.

"Aurora." It's my father's voice.

Hal and I jump apart.

Both of our faces are the color of my rose.

My parents and his are standing there.

How embarrassing, but what fun.

My mother smiles. "I'm very proud of you."

"Me too," my father says.

"We are too," the Brenners agree. "You were terrific, both of you."

Hal laughs. "Did you notice that the chairs were always in the right place? My job."

His father says, "I also noticed all the nights that you were up late working on the play."

Hal looks pleased.

"We have to go to the cast party," Hal reminds them.

We say good-bye to our parents and leave.

As Hal and I walk along, I think about how things have changed since I came to the moon. I know I'm going to have to make some important decisions soon.

But not tonight.

Tonight's a celebration.

33 _____

Dear Grandma Jennifer and Grandpa Josh,

This is not an easy letter to write.

I won't be coming back to earth this year after all. I've decided to graduate from Da Vinci School and to return to earth for college. It was not an easy decision, but I know it's the right one. I wouldn't fit in at my old school anymore. I'm also not sure that I want to make another change so soon, especially since I'm used to this place now and like a lot of people here more than I ever thought I could.

Also, the acting company is beginning and I really want to be an active member of it. I can't wait.

Another thing, for most of my life I've always thought that having a boyfriend was the most important thing in the world. Now I know there are a lot of other things that are also important. That doesn't mean that I don't care about Hal—I do. Actually, I care more about him than about any other boy I've ever gone out with. But who knows what will happen? For now, though, it's very special. (When you started going out with Grandpa, did your whole body

tingle? Does it still? This is the stuff that the sex-info
computer disk never discusses. I have a feeling I'm
getting ready to graduate to Disc II. I'm afraid to
think about what's on Disc V.)

The main reason I'm sorry I'm not coming home
right now is because I love and miss you so much. We
will see each other next year, though. I promise. I'm
absolutely, positively not staying up here forever.
This place really has no atmosphere. I still want to be
an actress and I need to see things and have experiences that I can't have up here. I've seen the moon.
Now I want to see Paris.

I guess that catches you up on just about everything I'm thinking about. Don't be too upset.

I'll be back on earth soon.

Maybe someday I'll be a star.

Today I'll just live among them.

                         Love,

Aurora D★☆★

♡ ♡ ♡ ♡ ♡ and XXXXXX

About the Author

PAULA DANZIGER flunked earth science in college, believing that the only rocks and minerals worth identifying were diamonds and amethysts.

Ms. Danziger lives in New York City and in Woodstock, New York. She has no plans to buy a moon condo or to "shuttle off to Buffalo."

Paula Danziger's humor and realistic prose have endeared her to a generation of readers. Her other books include *Can You Sue Your Parents for Malpractice?; The Cat Ate My Gymsuit; The Divorce Express; It's An Aardvark-Eat-Turtle World; The Pistachio Prescription;* and *There's a Bat in Bunk Five,* all available in Delacorte Press and Dell Laurel-Leaf editions.